BLOOD & THUNDER

Blood & Thunder

(Blood Rights, Book Two)

K. B. Thorne

To the women of my family who did not do a damn thing to teach me any 'traditional gender norms.' I'm not sure I even knew such 'norms' existed until I was an adult. Dakota is a testament to those of us who were out there building barns, planting fence posts, and moving that piece of furniture someone tried to tell us we shouldn't do on our own.

CHAPTER ONE

The problem with most people is that they're liars.

We all harbor a beast inside, and we all know it. Most people just won't admit it. That's why I like hunting animals. There's no duplicity. They are what they are.

The leafy trees of a New England forest in spring rushed past my feline ears as I raced after a non-human form preternatural. Also known as NHF, this meant I was chasing down an animal that had more speed, stamina, and strength than any 'regular' animal a person would generally encounter in their day-to-day lives.

In this instance, it was something like a wolf and roughly the size of a small pony. It had been terrorizing several suburban communities just outside of Adelheid with its very presence, and no one else wanted to tackle it, so they called me.

My name is Dakota. I hunt things. Not just any things, but preternatural things. Despite Cameron's Law making all us preternatural creatures legal citizens, there are still some who misbehave, so I hunt down the ones everyone else is afraid to, or isn't able to. I'm better at it than anyone else, so I get called a lot. It was my third NHF that month.

He knew I was right behind him. The scent of wolf, cougar, and magic was thick on the air. He followed the trail he thought would lead to freedom while I followed him. My preferred cat form was strong and fast. I liked cougar the best. It had a power to it many other forms, even bigger and brawnier animals, didn't have. It made me better at my job when I felt comfortable in the skin I wore.

Leaping over a fallen tree trunk, I landed in a pile of leaves that crunched under my paws, and the breeze shifted. I stopped abruptly and swung my head around, trying to pick up the scent I had suddenly lost. The forest was silent, and even the birds and insects were terrified by the sight of our chase. I stood perfectly still, and then I caught the sound of his crashing through the trees and took off once again.

I could tell he was growing tired. His steps slowed and lost their rhythmic pace. He'd be looking for a place to hide now, but there weren't any. I knew these woods well, and with the mind of a human. He didn't. Stumbling ahead of me, I caught sight of him and surged forward, leaping on his back and sending him sprawling with a snarl, all four feet slipping at different angles.

I rolled off and got back on my feet before he did. Already, I had shifted to my human form and pulled the tranquilizer gun off my belt. He lurched to his feet and leaped at me. I braced myself on one knee and fired. The dart caught him in the throat, just before he landed right out of bite range. His huge jaws snapped at me, and I danced back, waiting the few moments before the magically-enhanced drugs flooded his system and he collapsed in a heap of black fur at my feet.

I gazed down at the massive sleeping beast and sighed as I put the tranq gun away. This bastard was going to be heavy, but there was nothing for it. I bent down and pulled the huge frame across my shoulders and lifted with my knees. He *was* fucking heavy, even with all my strength, but I carried him through the woods, expertly following my tracks back to my car, where I piled the beastie in the back of the SUV and shut the hatch.

From there, everything was pretty easy. I drove him down to the office laughably called Animal Control. I say that because really it was just a place to house animals until they figured out what to do with them. They had no one qualified to catch them, except me, and were barely qualified to keep them. But there was nowhere else to go, so I dropped sleeping beauty off and got my signed receipt.

Then I went home.

Home was a studio apartment above a Chinese restaurant called the Golden Dragon. The apartment was owned by the same people who owned the restaurant. They gave me a good deal in exchange for helping with pest control, both human and animal. I could hunt mice or bounce drunks with equal skill.

I had been home all of an hour, resting and eating dinner, when my cell phone rang. I answered it…after a time. I'd decided to go with one of those new smart phones to help me conduct business better, but that didn't mean me and my phone actually got along.

"Hello?" I asked.

"Dakota." Stanton sounded exasperated.

Sadie Stanton owned the agency I worked for, although I wouldn't go so far as to call her my boss. I was an independent contractor. But no matter what you called us, she was always exasperated when she called me.

"What did I do *this* time?" I sighed and tried not to roll my eyes, already feeling like a teenager in trouble with their parents, which was funny when you considered that I was four times her age.

"Are you allergic to coming into the office and letting us know when you have a job finished?" she asked. "It came through us after all, and Madison likes to keep the files organized, so we need to know what's opened and what's closed."

Maybe I was allergic. Maybe I could get a doctor's note. "It was just an NHF. I didn't think it was that important."

She sighed. "I know you didn't. You never do, even if the hunt has twenty human forms. I think you just like pissing me off."

Getting to my feet to carry paper dishes to the trash, I snorted. "You got me," I said. "I just live to annoy you."

The long pause told me she wasn't impressed. "When you finish a hunt, come by or call and let us know. It's really not that difficult."

"Fine." I hung up without saying good-bye. Pleasantries were usually just a waste of time and air. I stuffed the phone back in my pocket. I had been working as the hunter for the Stanton Agency for a few months, and I still wasn't getting the hang of this shit, but their secretary handled a lot of the paperwork I hated and could sometimes be useful, so I was hanging in there anyways.

I and my aching muscles decided I'd worked enough for one night, and I threw myself onto my bed with my clothes on, asleep before I knew it.

☾○☽

The year is 1755.

I'm running through the forest. It's not the forests of America but of Europe more than two centuries ago. I'm not a cougar but a wolf. There is a deer leaping ahead of me, trying to get away from me, but I haven't eaten in days, and I need that deer. It's winter, and food is sparse. I have no intention of surviving everything I have just to starve to death now.

It flits around, zigzagging between trunks. I'm not at my best, and my steps are erratic, but I'm still quick. I reach the deer and bite at the backs of its legs, getting it to slow down. It's bleeding and stumbles. I'm on top of it, tearing into its throat until blood spurts in my mouth and it stops twitching. I grab it in my jaws and drag it back through the sticks and rocks till I reach the cave.

Hannah comes out. She's in wolf form, too. She eyes the

deer, and I don't have to ask to know what she's thinking. She's had more trouble handling the raw, recently-living meals than I've had...even after all this time. I think it's just ingrained now. I can't make it any easier on her, although I would if I could. She's my sister, after all, and I just want to take care of her. But I can't do everything, no matter how hard I try.

'Hexe, hexe...'

I hear a voice on the wind, but Hannah doesn't seem to notice. I must have heard nothing, so I shake it off. I close my eyes and say a quick prayer, trying to stop feeling everything that I'm feeling: the fear, the guilt... I try not to think, because now is not the time for thinking.

We both eventually tear into the animal's flesh because we are starving and there's nothing else. We're new in this area and don't know what plants are safe to eat, and there aren't many plants left now anyways. We have no home and no family, so no money, and we are too terrified to try to go into human society. It's too soon.

Eventually, we have eaten everything that can be eaten. Hannah looks like she feels as stuffed as I am, but we don't know when we'll eat again so it's best to make the most of it now, and so we do. Then, we slink to the back of the cave and curl up together.

What else is there to do?

❨○❩

The next day started like any other when I wasn't on the hunt, which was to say rather boring.

I got up and ate and showered. I took care of some paperwork from last night's hunt, and then I took care of some things around the house. By the time I was done, it was getting dark, and I decided I would be a good little soldier and go into the office. Generally speaking, I tried to avoid any place that held the name 'office,' but sometimes, there was no hiding. I had to check in and make sure Stanton wasn't foaming at the mouth about last night.

In truth, I wasn't really giving the woman enough credit. Blood suckers weren't my favorite, but she was a capable and level-headed creature, and she was a good boss, even if I wasn't exactly an employee. She was fair and considerate. In my more magnanimous moments, I thought she didn't really deserve all the shit I gave her, but those moments were thankfully rare.

Piling into my car, I wrinkled my nose at the lingering scent of dog that I could do nothing about and pulled onto the road. It was a little less than ten minutes till I pulled into a parking spot at the Stanton Agency and sauntered in. Madison, who was the secretary through the night shift, looked like she was just getting set up. This place was its busiest overnight, seeing as how the boss couldn't even get out of her daytime coma to come in until sunset, which was the case for many of our clients, too.

"Surprise, surprise," Madison said with the frighteningly sweet smile that said she really wanted to poke me with something sharp but was playing nice because that was her job. A passably pretty girl, werewolf, with blonde hair and big blue eyes, I always thought she looked like she should be in pigtails on a box of Swiss Miss rather than working in an office.

"Is Stanton in?" I knew the two of them lived together, so maybe they drove in together, too. I didn't like to call people by their first names unless I knew them really well, and I didn't get to know people that well that often. Some people I couldn't help it with, though, like Madison.

Madison nodded. "She is," she said. "She also happens to be free at the moment and, as far as I know, isn't on the phone. So, if you feel like putting your head in the bear's mouth, you can go on in."

I gave her a dry look. "I like bears," I muttered with fervor, walking past her desk and into the office behind her.

"I'd be mad at you for not knocking if I wasn't just so bowled over that you actually decided to grace us with your presence," Stanton said before I even had both feet over the threshold. I paused, batting down a serious urge to turn around and walk right back out because she was a smartass. "Shut the door."

"This must be what it's like for school kids that get called into the principal's office," I commented.

That wasn't something I had firsthand knowledge in, but I could guess it felt something like this. I shut the door and sat down. She hadn't invited me to sit, but I did it anyways. Contrary to what most people thought, I actually did know what was proper and in keeping with manners in most situations. I just chose to ignore it.

Stanton folded her hands on the edge of her desk and leaned forward. That was when I knew this was going to be an oh-so-fun speech. It was taking her too long to get the first words together.

"I know that our arrangement isn't exactly employer and employee," she began, and I already knew this. I considered not listening but resisted the rebelliousness. "You work in a profession that has you working alone. I get that you're just contracted to work with us, but in doing so, you aren't an island."

"I'm never an island," I pointed out. "I don't have the mass for it."

Her mouth twitched. She wanted to laugh. I could tell. Her self-restraint impressed me, however. "If you are going to work with us, then there are some times you are going to have to do just that: work with us, and you'll have to do it whether you like it or not. Because, sometimes, grown-ups have to do things we don't like, and I know you're about twenty times older than the rest of us, so you should be better at it."

"Hey." I frowned. She knew how old I was. She was just goading me. I hated when she did that because she was really fucking good at it sometimes. "I think my age grants me the right to *not* do anything I don't want to do."

"Doesn't work that way," she told me without missing a beat. "You're a damn good hunter, and I don't want to lose you. Having you on the letterhead, so to speak, brings in a lot more business in the hunting game. I also sometimes even like you as a person, when you're not being a pain in the ass. That's not often, but sometimes. I'd like for you to continue working with us, but you will have to do the team thing some of the time, which means keeping us in the loop better, for one."

I looked around, plotting my escape. "I can work on it." This definitely had to be what it felt like to get called into the principal's office. "Just don't nag me."

She shrugged, looking unimpressed. "I'll nag you when it needs doing, but if you work with us as needed and keep doing your job, then I won't have to hound you."

"I suppose so," I said. I hated giving up ground just on principle, really, but I knew she was kind of right.

The fact of the matter was that I did sort of like working with the agency. Madison was very good at her job, and her job saved me from a lot of things I loathed, like the paperwork, but also customer service and appointment-making. I would rather be out on the road or in the woods, doing the actual tracking and hunting and catching.

"Are we done?" I asked.

"Yeah." She nodded. "Go see Madison. She has a job for you."

Chapter Two

Madison didn't seem to have much to say to me, which I supposed I couldn't blame her for. She told me that Rikki Myles was looking for me and that I ought to meet with her tonight because she wanted to hire me. There was a bad guy to catch, and after turning in the Big Bad Wolf, my dance card was open.

Rikki Myles was the owner of Myles Bail-Bonds. Hers was one of those businesses that straddled the divide between the humans and preternaturals because she took on jobs for either kind. The only difference was who she sent after them when they skipped. She sent humans after humans, and she sent me after the rest, at least the big ones. The lightweight crimes didn't get my phone ringing, but a preternatural with a heavy indictment on them did. I got the violent offenders. Lucky me.

Her secretary, a short firecracker of a blonde named Sandra, who I still didn't believe wasn't from New Jersey, showed me back to the office. I sat down and waited for Myles to tell me about the job. My eyes briefly wandered around the room, taking in the small shield and crossed shortswords behind her desk, which I found an interesting choice, along with the other various artistic renderings. The general theme seemed to be...strong women. I could appreciate that.

I turned back to her. She was an attractive woman in her late thirties, with short dark hair and dark eyes, a psychic but of weak power, and I didn't know what kind, just a couple of inches shorter than me. I chose to be six foot in this form. She got it naturally. Of course, the one thing that stood out was that she only had one breast and didn't bother to hide it. She was reading something on the computer screen that made her frown, and I briefly wondered what it was.

"Sorry about that," she said, turning and flashing me a smile. "Thanks for coming. If you were much later, I wouldn't have been here. My group is meeting tonight." I knew she was a breast cancer survivor and had a rather special support group, but I didn't know much about her past that. "I've got a vampire on the run from manslaughter charges." She also didn't waste time, which was something I appreciated.

"What's the story?" I asked.

"She got into a fight and won," Myles replied. "That's really the basic story and about as much as I have on the matter." She pulled a folder from the top of a pile on her desk and handed it to me.

I opened it and felt my breath hitch in my throat when I saw the name. Swallowing hard, I forced myself to remain my usual charming self as I looked up. "Carrie Stone?" I asked. I wanted to make sure I had read this right, that this was the person she wanted me to hunt.

Myles nodded. She watched me carefully. "I believe you're previously acquainted with Ms. Stone?" The look in her eye told me she already knew the answer. It was just social protocol that made her ask. I didn't appreciate that as much.

"Yes," I said flatly. I wondered how she knew. Myles and I had worked together several times in the past, but I couldn't imagine ever mentioning Carrie. "We were romantically involved for a time." I wasn't going to tell her any more than that.

"Can you handle the hunt?" she asked.

"Yes."

She eyed me for a long moment and then nodded. "All right," she said. "It's yours, but if you have any trouble, please don't hesitate to talk to me about it, okay?"

I frowned. "Okay," I said. I wasn't used to people making that offer, or insisting on something like that, but okay. "I'll be in touch soon." I left.

I walked to my car but had to stop when I felt that twitchy feeling between the shoulder blades, like someone was watching me. I wasn't sure how I knew, but after a few centuries of always looking over my shoulder, I kind of had a sense of these things. I stood in front of my car door and looked around. There were people milling in front of stores across the street. I thought I saw someone, a man, staring at me, but then he was gone with the crowd. Maybe I hadn't seen anything.

I got in the car and drove off.

☾O☽

I went back to my apartment. There was an office down at the agency with my name on the door, but I didn't like using it.

Sitting on the floor with a legal pad and a pen, I began writing down everything I could remember about Carrie. I tried to think of her as just another failure-to-appear but knew that wasn't going to work. She wasn't just another stranger I could think bad things about and hunt down. I already knew I wouldn't get any satisfaction in catching and hauling her to the police station.

I wrote down what I knew.

Carolyn Stone, also known as Carrie

Born in autumn of 1779 as Marie-Jeanne Portefaix

Parents died during French Revolution

** Orphan living on the streets of Paris until she was turned into a vampire at the age of nineteen*

** Name of her sire is unknown. She never told me. Hinted he was old. Lived with him until she immigrated to the United States in the early 1900s*

** Lived in several cities from New York to California and back to the East Coast in the late 1990s*

I met her after she moved to Adelheid in 2008, and we started dating shortly after that. It lasted a little over a year. I remember how intense she was, and beautiful. Her face was shaped between a square and a heart, enough of the former to be unique but of the latter to be feminine, with eyes drifting up at the corners in a way that was vaguely cat-like. I suppose that was what appealed to me the most at first.

Blue eyes. I stared a long time into those eyes, wondering what was behind their perpetual mischief. Inside of a year, I had never figured it out, and she left me so suddenly and so completely that I never had the chance to again.

Maybe I would get that chance now.

I opened the file folder and looked over reports. She was arrested in the apartment of a woman named Natalia Winters. Winters, a human, was dead. Both bodies and the living room looked like there had been a fight, which was what Carrie confirmed in her statement to the police afterward. The two women had fought over money. That sounded ridiculous right away, because Carrie—like many vampires who had saved over their long lives with less expenses than humans—wasn't dependent from paycheck to paycheck like most people.

Humans usually stand little chance against vampires, so Winters predictably lost, but things went too far, and she ended up dead. The police had been called on a noise complaint, so they arrived just at the end of things. Carrie was arrested and released on a high bail, which was done through Myles's company.

Now, she had vanished. Myles would be out a lot of money if I didn't bring her back.

"Carrie," I sighed. "What in the hell did you get yourself into?"

A strong, stabbing feeling pressed inside my chest. I knew what it was right away, but I didn't want to acknowledge it. The pain was too old. I didn't want to think about it but had the idea I'd not have much say in the matter soon.

I tried to ignore the feeling and kept looking through her file. The basic information they had for her home address and place of work was the same as when we had broken up, which would make things a little simpler to start out. I didn't expect them to stay that way, because they never did when I was chasing anything with a human-like mind. Animals were simpler. Humans and anything like them were complicated, which made them annoying.

There was no time like the present to get started.

☾O☽

I drove to her apartment building on the other side of town. Seeing the building rising into the night sky brought a keen sense of longing and memories. The stabbing feeling returned. I felt betrayed, even though we had been broken up for a while, and her crime had absolutely nothing to do with me. The fact that she had committed a crime and landed on my doorstep made me feel betrayed anyways.

There was nothing for it, so I got out of the car and walked up to the building. It was supposed to be one you had to be buzzed into, but I tried the door and found that the lock was broken. So, I pulled open the lawsuit-waiting-to-happen and walked in, found her door, and tried that handle. It was also unlocked. If this were a novel or movie, I would expect this was way too easy, and I was walking into some overly dramatized trap.

Seeing as how it was real life, I decided there wasn't a serial killer in a hockey mask inside, and in I went.

What struck me was how much it had changed. Of course, I didn't have any reason to expect that everything would be exactly the same, but this was completely altered into decorating that I never, in a million years, would have expected from Carrie. I saw floral patterns in shades of mauve and lilac everywhere. Carrie was a vampire's vampire, down to the stereotypical décor, which meant dark and gothic. Not this.

I poked around. I was supposed to be looking for a hint of where Carrie was now, but I found myself looking for any trace of where she had been in this apartment.

Behind me, the doorknob turned. I whirled around and tensed. Could I really be so lucky as to have Carrie deliver herself into my hands? I was ready to jump, but the door opened, and a woman I had never seen before stepped inside.

She looked up and saw me. We had that long *what the fuck* moment, staring at one another, before she started screaming. I didn't catch all of it, but the important parts were things like "help" and "there's someone in my house" and "who the hell are you" and various statements of that nature. My plan of attack changed abruptly to a plan of escape, which led me right out the window, breaking glass on my way.

Hawk wings slowed my descent, and I caught the breeze into a convenient nearby tree, where I found a branch and watched what followed.

It didn't take long for a black-and-white police cruiser to pull up. Lights went on and off through the broken window. I caught a glimpse of a uniformed officer and the woman I scared the hell out of. The report didn't take very long. I hadn't touched anything but the doorknob (which probably had lots of prints) or taken anything, so there wasn't much to make note of and no stand-out prints. The woman would have seen my face, but only briefly. With the dim light and the fright, she probably wouldn't even remember.

I waited, ruffling my feathers because I could, until the police car left. Once they had, I flew down to the ground and retook human form to get into my car. Once behind the wheel, I just sat there for a while.

Two possibilities came to mind. Either Carrie had a new roommate who was a slave driver when it came to decorating and took it all over, or she didn't live there anymore. It was a fifty-fifty shot. The latter was a blow to the case because it made it a little bit harder, but the former was a blow to the ego. It had been more than a year, but that didn't mean I liked the idea of her living with someone else.

My phone rang. I didn't know how long I'd been sitting, wrestling with myself, before it did, but I didn't like it.

"Yeah," I answered it like a bored businessman.

"You'll never guess who I talked to tonight." Stanton didn't sound happy. "I got a call from the cops. It felt a little like a parent who gets called into the principal's office about an errant child."

Funny, I knew a little about how that felt...but what's more, I had a bad feeling about where this was headed. Damn, they worked fast.

"Are you listening?"

"Yes, mother, what can I do for you?" I drawled.

There was a long pause. And there was no breathing from the other side the whole time because vampires are creepy fuckers. "The cops called me with a B and E report they took just this evening. One of the uniforms had the pleasure of meeting you in the past and thought he recognized the description. Since it's vague and nothing was taken, they'll agree to not lock you away."

"I'll pay for the window," I muttered.

"Is that a confession?"

I thought that over. "A charitable gesture?"

"Anyone who knows you wouldn't fall for it, but we'll call it that to keep your ass out of jail." She paused. "Do I have to remind you that breaking and entering is kind of frowned on? I know that bounty hunters get a pretty big margin of error, but let's get serious here. The goodwill of the police will not stretch everywhere. I'm dating a cop and would still get locked up if I broke into someone's house."

"I'm not going to comment on your sex life, but obviously, you're not doing it right."

There was another breathless pause, and I realized that I probably should have kept my mouth shut. "Do you really think now is the time to be a smartass?"

"I gave it a shot."

"Stop breaking into places. If I have to call you again and yell at you, we're going to make sure it's really unpleasant."

"And I was having so much fun."

The call ended.

Maybe I shouldn't have been such a jackass, but it wasn't like I could change it, so I'd just have to live with her disappointment. I had gotten pretty good at it over the past few months.

Regardless, I still had a job to do.

Sliding out of my car, I shifted to a new face. This body was shorter and more feminine, because I had found that was less intimidating. I made myself cute, with red hair and blue eyes, a form that would make me sick if I had to live in it.

I went back into the building, but this time looking for the manager. He was in his office on the first floor with the door open. He looked middle-aged and smelled like a human. I smiled and knocked on the door frame.

Startled, his head popped up, but then his weathered

face smiled and dark eyes glinted with surprise. Maybe there weren't a lot of cute girls dropping by his office to chat. That would work in my favor.

"What can I do for you?"

"I'm trying to find an old friend of mine," I said with my best damsel-in-distress, please-sir-can-you-help-me smile. "We fell out of touch for a while, and I tried calling her number, but I never get through. I know she used to live here, though I can't for the life of me remember the apartment number. Carrie Stone, do you know her?"

He rubbed his two day's growth of beard. I knew he'd want to help me, if he could. "I seem to remember a woman by that name," he said thoughtfully. "I think she moved out, oh, going on a year back now. Someone else lives in that apartment."

I sighed dramatically, shoulders rising and falling in a pronounced gesture. "This is why you should never fall out of touch with your friends. A year gone by, and I don't know where she's living now. Pity, pity." I shook my head.

"I can't give you a forwarding address, darling." He smiled apologetically. "Though, I'm not sure I even have one to give or not."

"Oh, that's all right," I said with a wave of my hand. "It's my own fault."

"Don't know if you'll have much luck finding her now," he added after a moment. "I recall some cops coming by a few months ago, asking about her. They didn't tell me what it was about, but maybe she's in some kind of trouble."

I frowned like this news surprised and disconcerted me. "Oh, I hope not. Well, I guess I'll just have to keep trying and see if I can dig anything up." I was tempted to see if I could get any information out of him about the apartment and the break-in, but I didn't want to draw too much attention to myself. "Thanks anyways." I tossed him a small smile and wave, leaving quickly.

❲O❳

I didn't bother putting my usual face back on as I drove from the apartment building to where Carrie had worked, last I knew. After learning she had moved out of her apartment without telling anyone or anyone seeming to know where she went, I had little hope of learning anything useful at the computer company where she worked as the overnight customer service person.

When I got there, I put on the same routine for the receptionist as I'd given the apartment building manager, and I got the same reply. She had quit about a year ago. This time, I was re-directed to a man she had apparently been friendly with.

"You're looking for Carrie?" he asked when I got to his cubicle. He looked like the quintessential IT guy who never got out in the sun and preferred glasses to contacts. His dark hair might have been brushed last week, but I doubt it had seen his comb since.

"That's right." I flashed my perfect smile. A good show of lips and teeth, tilted in the right direction, could keep a lot of people from being annoyed about curt word choices.

"Join the club." He pulled his headset off and set it on the desk. "No one has been able to reach her since she quit. I'd say it was a shame, but she changed in the couple of weeks before she just left. She was real friendly with people before, nice and all, but then she turned inward at the drop of a hat." He pulled his glasses off, idly cleaning them with the hem of his T-shirt. He showed less reaction to my cute appearance than I would have expected from a presumably girl-starved human male. "And then there were some cops looking for her, but no one said what that was about."

The story he told me of Carrie was a familiar one. It wasn't that I had heard it before. I had lived it.

"And no one had any idea what happened? Or about the cops?" I asked. The perplexed look I wore was not difficult to achieve sincerely. "I mean, she kind of just disappeared on me too, so I guess I shouldn't be surprised, but still. I wonder what happened. I hope she's not in any kind of trouble.

He nodded, slipping his glasses back on. "So did all of us," he agreed. "If you ever find out, let me know, would you?"

I smiled sadly. "You bet."

I walked away from this new dead end. As I walked out, I was left with the big lingering question: what the hell happened a year ago?

Chapter Three

Checking home and work off my mental list, I went to the next place I knew Carrie used to spend a lot of time: 5. It had been an 'underground' haven for vampires and the supernatural before legalization. Now it was just another vampire bar.

I found a parking spot toward the back and made my way in. It had started its life as a two-story Victorian and still looked like it on the outside. The owner had converted the first floor into a bar and the upper level into his apartment. He was, of course, a vampire, so he didn't need much by way of amenities. I didn't know him well but had spoken with him on occasion.

"Haven't seen you in a while," Quintus greeted me as I came up to the bar. He sniffed the air dramatically. "Don't smell like you joined the blood-sucking crowd either."

He was a giant of a man. I chose to be tall, but he lived at about 6'6" all the time and seemed nearly as wide. His skin was so dark he almost blended into the bar's barely-there light. Vampires like the dark, after all. Even to my exceptional sight, sometimes all I could see were flashes of white teeth and the whites of his eyes. I always thought he did it on purpose. I suspected he liked freaking people out.

"The nose knows, eh?" I folded my arms along the bar and leaned in. "I'm here looking for someone."

"Everyone is looking for someone." He poured a glass of the red stuff and slid it to the eternal 'lonely heart' at the end that every place like this came equipped with. The metallic scent lingered even after the glass was gone. "Isn't that what I'm supposed to say? You know I'll help if I can, though you really should consider helping me out sometime."

I grimaced. I should have known he would bring this up. "I'm sorry, Quintus, but it just makes me feel very strange."

He shrugged massively. "It would be good money. I'll bet no vampire bar in the world would have your vintage in stock. I could charge a bundle for just a shot of it, and you know us dead boys and girls got the cash laying around for it."

The idea of his having a bottle of my blood on hand to sell to his patrons was still more than I could bear. I imagined he was right, but it was still creepy. And coming from me, that was saying a lot. "Try me again next time. I'm here working."

"Me too." His smile flashed big enough to see the long ones, too.

Few in the world were as good at talking me in circles as he was, but I knew that he was centuries older than I. That had something to do with it, I was sure.

"I used to come here with a woman, a little over a year ago." I charged ahead, because it was the only way I was going to get anywhere. "Her name is Carrie Stone, and she's part of your crowd. Do you remember her?"

"Of course," he replied easily. His tree trunk arms folded over his chest. "She still came in here after you two stopped coming together. I saw her just a few weeks ago, before she fell off the radar. I heard she got in some kind of trouble with the law, which I figure is the reason for her vanishing."

The thought that she had been here more recently than a year was enough to give me some hope for a lead. I didn't let my minimal excitement show. "That's about the whole of it." I considered my next questions carefully. "Did she ever give any indication about where she was staying lately? She moved out of the apartment I knew a year ago."

His pause was long, leaving me to wait until he spoke again, with nothing to take in but the occasional dull murmur of voices and the heady, salty scent of blood. "Is this professional, or are you trying to track down an old girlfriend?"

"Which one is more likely to get my question answered?" I smiled by half.

He chuckled. It was a deep rumbling sound, like thunder in the distance. "I don't really know," he said. "I hate to be the one to give anyone up, but I also don't aim to be standing in the way of the law when shit's gone down. Either way, though, I can't tell you. She never told me where she was staying, and she always paid in cash."

There went my little lead. I sighed. "Do you guys get turned with instant knowledge of how to hide your asses from the rest of the world?"

"No, but we learn fast," he said. "I can tell you that there was a woman she spent a lot of time talking to. I know you and Carrie were pretty tight, so I don't want you going on some jealous rampage through my bar. Not that most of my patrons would mind if you left a few bloody body parts behind, but I would certainly care. I don't want to be the one who has to clean it up, after all."

I wasn't sure if I was offended or not, but I didn't have time to be. "I promise I will play nice." I was making this promise a lot these days, it seemed. I didn't know what to think about that, either. "Does this woman come in here often enough that I might have a chance to talk to her?"

"She's here now." He pointed to the 'lonely heart.'

I looked at her and frowned, inhaling deeply. It was hard to cut through the blood scent, but eventually I did. I turned back to Quintus. "She's human. How is she not swamped by you guys in here?"

Even in the darkness, I could tell his expression was not amused. "We do have some self-control. She never talked to anyone but Carrie. I'm not sure why she still comes here, now that Carrie doesn't anymore."

When I looked at the woman again, I tried to imagine why Carrie had been talking to her so much, enough to be noticed. She wasn't any great beauty, but then neither was I. All I could tell was average height and weight, but in good shape. Everything looked dark in this light, so I couldn't be sure of her race or what color her hair was. All I knew was she wasn't as dark as Quintus because I could see her facial features, mostly.

I tried to keep any emotional reaction suitably locked away as I turned back to him. "Do you know her name?"

"No," he said. "Like I said, she doesn't talk to anyone except to order."

"You gave her a glass of blood, but she's human." This connection had taken me a moment to put together.

He shrugged. With shoulders that size, I suppose shrugging a lot was a given. "I don't ask questions like that. She can do as she wants, as long as she pays for it."

That sounded a lot like my business policy, so I could hardly fault him. It didn't help me much, but this was the most information I had gotten during my entire evening's worth of work, so I had to go with it. For some reason, I was glad I was wearing my usual form now, although I had no idea why.

"Thanks," I tossed to Quintus as I pushed away from the bar and walked the few seats down to the human. I sat beside her. "Hey."

She turned her head and looked at me. It was a look that took a long time to perfect and had I just been looking for a hook-up, I would have taken it as the instant rebuff it was and gone on my way. Since my motives were quite different, however, I didn't leave. She stared at me a moment longer, like she was waiting for me to do just that.

When it was clear I wasn't going anywhere, she turned away without a word and looked into the still-full glass between her hands.

"I'm looking for a woman named Carrie Stone." I decided to try a more direct approach.

It caught her attention enough that she looked at me again with less reserve but snapped her head away immediately. I could see the tension in her shoulders, and now her staring into the glass was more focused, trying to shut me out specifically instead of just shutting out everything in general. I had seen this look before.

Resting an elbow on the edge of the counter, I leaned into it like I didn't care about the look she gave me. And it was the truth. I could beat anybody's bad attitude. Or just beat them.

"I can sit here until Hell freezes over," I said plainly. "I know you've talked to her on more than one occasion, so you might as well tell me what you know."

"I didn't talk to the cops when they found me, so why would I talk to you?" She still wasn't looking at me. I found myself a little surprised the cops had already talked to her, but then I chastised myself for that. This bar was listed as a known location in Carrie's file, after all, and I was sure Quintus would have told them what he'd told me. He didn't want trouble.

"I'm not a cop." I stated the obvious. "I need to find her."

She shrugged, but her shoulders were less impressive than the bartender's. "I don't care. I don't have anything to say to you." Her shoulders curved inward like a shield against me.

I considered continuing to throw myself at the brick wall sitting beside me but decided it probably wouldn't be in my best interest. I might be able to find her again later if I had to, or I might not. I didn't think she would tell me her name if I asked, so I didn't bother trying.

With a nod at Quintus, I made my way out.

☾O☽

From there, I went home.

I wasn't really sure what I was feeling, because there were too many things going on at once. It was far too early to be frustrated with a job, but I was. I think that had more to do with the target than the results thus far. It wasn't until I was driving home that it hit me, the weight of who I was chasing.

Had Carolyn Stone been the great love of my life? I didn't know, but I did know I was pretty head over heels for her when I had never felt that way before. Then it had all ended so abruptly. That kind of sudden end after dramatic emotion leaves quite the wound. And in a life as long as mine, wounds last a long time. And can tear open very easily.

Reaching the top of my stairs, I was finding my house key when I caught a strange scent lingering before my door, like someone had been standing there for a while. Each nerve stood up, and I froze, inhaling deeply. There was something vaguely familiar about the scent, but I couldn't place it. It wasn't a vampire, so it wasn't Carrie or Stanton. The smell was similar to an animal, but no animal I recognized quickly. It wasn't a werewolf.

I turned my head to the door and examined the knob, the lock, and the edges with great care, but I didn't see any evidence of a break-in. I had wards drawn by fae on the inside to prevent someone from using magic to get inside and I didn't feel their warning, so I felt confident no one had broken in. That was almost worse, though, because it meant someone came to my door and stood there. Doing what, I had to wonder.

It wasn't like there was such a thing as door-to-door salesmen anymore, and the last Jehovah's Witness had to have told everyone to never stop at my door again after what I did to him. He had lived to tell the tale, but I made certain he'd been scared out of his wits.

Unlocking my door, I cautiously entered. The familiar scent didn't follow inside, but I thoroughly examined every corner of my place anyways. I had little of value, but everything remained where it should be. Nothing was missing, and nothing was disturbed. Except me, of course, but that eased, and I settled in.

It didn't last long. My phone rang. It was Myles.

"Calling to check up on me so soon? I'd be offended if I cared."

"You're always a pleasure to talk to, Dakota." Myles was unperturbed by my attitude, as usual. "I'm actually calling to relay a bit of information."

That got my attention. "A tip about Carrie?" What else could it be?

"Yep. She was spotted just a couple of weeks ago, after she got out on bail, in a bar downtown called Phoenix."

Another bar? Jesus. All vampires had a tendency to be lushes, but it seemed like the only places she had been in a year were bars. "I'll check it out." I didn't want to tell Myles too much just yet. It wasn't a matter of trust so much as, well, it was a matter of trust, but I didn't trust anyone, so it wasn't personal.

We hung up. Some belated voice within suggested I should have thanked her, but I ignored it and went about my business.

I would check out Phoenix tomorrow night. First, I was going to see if I could wrestle information out of any of Carrie's last known friends. Almost all of them were vampires, so I knew they'd be awake at this hour. I had a list of about four people, and all the names were familiar to me.

Unfortunately, every conversation went about the same.

"Hi, it's Dakota. Do you remember me? I was a friend of Carrie's."

"Yes, I remember you."

"I'm trying to get in touch with Carrie. Have you seen her lately?"

"No, can't say that I have. She sort of just fell off the face of the planet about a year ago, I think. And I think she got arrested recently, didn't she? Don't know what happened there."

"Yeah, me neither."

I threw the phone at the other end of the couch. What was Carrie playing at? One of the things I had liked about her was that she didn't play the games many vampires her age did, but this felt like one to me. She had to be living somewhere. Perhaps she had enough savings to not work, but she had to have a roof to keep her body out of the sun during the day. Could she really be doing nothing but spending time in bars? I was as much a fan of bars as anyone, but it sounded ridiculous.

There seemed to be little else to do, so I went to bed.

☾ O ☽

The year is 1883.

I'm standing in the shadows of an alley. From around the edge of a stone building, I can see her in the street. She looks very nice in her human clothes, which are a big improvement over the rags we had been accustomed to wearing, that I was still wearing. I blend in effortlessly with the other vagabonds of a London street, only I'm not looking for food or coin or shelter.

I'm looking for her.

Hannah has changed her appearance a little. She looks older than she did when she left me. Her blonde hair is swept up in the fashion of the other ladies I see walking the streets, and her dress is, as well. I wonder if she formed herself with those clothes or found some employment to buy them. The former takes a lot of effort, but the latter can be tricky too, I know.

Then again, we had been living in the wild for so long. How did I know anything at all, if I even knew it in the first place?

She is laughing. She is shopping. I watch her as she browses a vendor's cart, picking up items I can't make out the details of, examining each one and then putting it away before moving onto the next. How does she blend in so seamlessly? How did she become a part of the human world with so little apparent effort?

How could she leave me? She didn't know. I had never been able to confess to her my sins...

There is a man standing beside her. At first, I think he is just there. Perhaps he is with someone else, or is just taking a moment's pause. Then I realize she is looking at him, and the smiles and laughs are for him. I desperately want to know who he is. I want to know who she has fallen in with so quickly, but I can't make out his face. He never turns in my direction, so all I ever see is the back of his head and the reactions he gets out of her.

I don't understand. It breaks my heart, but all I can do is watch until I shift into a rat and scurry away, back to the safety of the woodlands.

CHAPTER FOUR

My damn phone was ringing. Alarm clocks are terrible enough, but waking to a ringing phone seems even more obnoxious. Perhaps it is the lack of control. A ringing phone is someone else deciding you have slept enough rather than making your own decision when setting a clock. Whatever it was, my phone was ringing and I was unhappily awake.

I groped around the nightstand for the chirping technological monstrosity. "Yeah?"

"This is Detective Marlowe with the Adelheid Police."

I first thought they were calling about the break-in at Carrie's apartment, but I thought that had been settled. Either way, she had my interest. I sat up and scrubbed my free hand over my face. "What can I do for you, Detective?" It was about as much civility as I could manage without being awake longer. That was a lie. It was about as much civility as I cared to manage any time.

"Would you come down to the station at your earliest convenience?" Nykk Marlowe was perhaps the only person in the world who could achieve less emotion in her voice than me, at least of anyone I ever met.

If this was about the apartment building, I doubt they would be so polite. Even so, I couldn't guess why they would be calling otherwise. "What's this about?"

She dodged my question artfully. "We'd prefer to discuss that when you arrive. Can you come down today?"

"I suppose so. I'll be there in—" I checked the time. "—an hour."

"We'll see you then." She hung up.

I tossed my phone back on the nightstand. Using up my hour, I showered, dressed, and had breakfast. I got to the police station with a few minutes to spare and was met at the front desk by Marlowe. Her expression and the red scarring on her face made her as dour a greeter as every time I'd seen her in the past. "Follow me," she said simply, so I did.

We walked through the squad room. Nothing had changed since the last time I was here, though I tried to keep those visits limited. However, after a few moments, I did spot one face that I hadn't seen before sitting at a desk in the back.

"New detective?" I asked Marlowe. It was one of those rare occasions when my curiosity got the better of me. It was kind of hard not to. The woman was gorgeous, but not in any of the typical ways, with a long face and nose that may have been broken a time or two. There was something exotic about a heritage I couldn't easily pin down, and the long curve of her neck into her jacket.

Marlowe followed my line of sight. "That's Samantha Moore. She's from Hartford and is here borrowing a desk while working on a case that led here." That was as much as I was going to get out of her, apparently, because she turned and kept walking.

I followed, but my gaze drifted a few more times back to the detective. At one point before I was led into the captain's office, she lifted her eyes and met mine. The door shut and ended that moment, and that's when I realized just what room I was in. Naturally, I didn't let my surprise show but inwardly, I couldn't imagine what was going on. The question was enough to drive the beautiful woman outside quite from my thoughts.

Captain Roy was not a very big man, but he filled the room well enough, with dark skin and short balding hair.

Marlowe's partner, Detective Vance Johnston (a solidly built, golden-eyed weretiger, and my boss's boyfriend) was already in there. The two of them lingered at the edges of the room. It was Roy who took my attention.

"I'm sure that you must be wondering why we called you in here," he began.

"It had occurred to me."

"Very simply put, Ms. Dakota, we need your help." He pulled a file folder off the top of a considerable stack on his full desk. "We want to hire you."

I looked from him to the two detectives standing against the wall. It was true that I only knew them a little, but that was more than I knew Roy. They all seemed earnest. My attention slid back to the captain. "I would have thought you'd have heard I'm already on a case, hired by Myles Bail-Bonds."

He nodded. "We know."

"I don't do two hunts at once." I suppose I had to give it to them that they might not have known that, but I thought it would have been obvious. Your average human bounty hunter might be able to work more than one case at a time, but when you were after creatures like us, you were doing the world a disservice to let your attention be split until you had the bad guys off the street.

"Would you consider making an exception?" Johnston asked.

I looked at him and then back again. "No."

The captain steepled his fingers in front of him. If I had been his employee, I might have been concerned for the trouble I was getting into. As I wasn't, I didn't worry too much. "I hope you will reconsider," he said. "Quite frankly, you may be our only option."

"There are other hunters," I pointed out carefully, though even as I said the words, I felt like I was about to be backed into a corner.

"None with your experience or success rate," he replied.

I didn't like corners, but I got the definite impression from the look on his face that this wasn't going to be let go easily. I could at least hear them out, but I really didn't like the idea of taking on two jobs at once.

"What's the hunt?" I finally asked. I sat down now because it was clear this wasn't going to be over with as quickly as I had hoped. "I'm not agreeing to anything."

Roy put the file down in front of me, but I didn't pick it up. That felt like too much of a concession. "His name is Anselmo De Laurentis."

"At least that's what he goes by now," Johnston pointed out. "The last name, as far as we can tell, remains the same. He just changes his first name."

"He's a vampire," Roy continued. "The reason we require a very skilled hunter is because he's an ancient."

That got my attention. I arched a brow. "Are you certain?"

Roy nodded. He knew just how heavy a piece of information that was. "By all the information we have, he is over a thousand years old."

"Now, that's interesting." I smiled. I've often been told it's a disquieting expression, which was never a good enough reason for me to alter it. In fact, I kind of liked it. "I've never hunted an ancient before." The challenge was quite alluring, and yet I still had my rules about two hunts at once for a reason. "What's he done?"

"Thus far, the squad room is collectively comparing him to a mob boss," Marlowe supplied, "but I think perhaps crime lord is more accurate."

Roy nodded. "We've linked him to several crimes in the area, from burglary to assault, and he's suspected in a couple of murders. He doesn't work very hard to conceal his involvement but by all accounts, he doesn't often commit crimes himself. He gets others to do it."

Johnston chimed in. "Cult leader is another term bandied about."

"Yes, and while we can make the connections, with evidence strong enough for an arrest and indictment, we face two issues. First of all, he doesn't hide his involvement, but he does hide himself, and he knows how to do it very well. Secondly, we are simply not equipped to handle a vampire of his age and potential power."

"I'd imagine not," I said thoughtfully. "You do realize, of course, that the chances of bringing in an ancient alive are slim at best."

"We are aware of that," Roy replied. "So is the state's attorney, but our options are few to none, and our evidence is compelling enough to warrant hiring you, if you'll take the job."

I didn't reply right away. I had to think about it, balancing out things in my head. It would be like playing two games of chess simultaneously. I didn't doubt my abilities but had to figure out if I wanted to cause myself the headache.

Johnston broke through my reverie. "We need the help, Dakota. Sadie says you're the best she's ever seen."

Turning my head, I eyed him. "Flattery doesn't go far with me, Detective." I paused and then sighed. "But I'll take your case anyway." The challenge was too much to resist. Besides, it never hurt to have friends in the police. I picked up the folder.

"Do *try* to bring him in alive," Roy said.

"I always do and always have," I replied, standing. But, admittedly, this would be a first for me. "Anything else?"

Roy shook his head. "Keep me apprised."

☾O☽

As I didn't want to get called into the principal's office again, I called the office and left a message. I kept it short and just told them the police had hired me for a second case, and I'd accepted.

I went back home. I sat down at the table to look through the folder I had been given.

Likely born somewhere in the Byzantine Empire, around 990 or 1000 A.D.

Birth name unknown, has gone by De Laurentis in all known records

Known to be in the British Isles somewhere during the 1800s

Known to be in the United States by the 1960s

Crimes begin roughly five years ago, starting small and getting bigger with several armed robberies, assaults, protection rackets and, finally, dead bodies

There wasn't much. Like with any vampire that old, it was a lot of "known to be" and "believed to be" notes through the whole file.

Given his age and chosen name, I guessed he had been the son of Laurentius and had chosen his name to reflect that. Some vampires could be very sentimental. There was nothing about his sire, the one who created him, but I wasn't surprised. I *was* surprised there was anything about him in the first place.

Some of their information came from people who had been arrested in crimes De Laurentis had directed. They had confessed, but then apparently all became babbling idiots that even court psychologists couldn't crack. They went to mental hospitals rather than prison. It was enough to point fingers, so to speak, but not much use in knowing how to find and capture the vampire. Then again, his status as an ancient would have made that near impossible even if they had been more helpful.

There was an address where they knew he had lived at one point but didn't believe he lived there anymore. At least, they'd found no evidence of it. There was no work history, but that wasn't uncommon for older vampires and, besides, he was living a life of crime, so why bother to work legitimately?

I did wonder about the timeline, because I doubted a vampire of that age would wait until he was over a thousand to start breaking the law. It was more likely that he had never been tagged with any previous crimes, but why stop being sneaky now? It didn't make a whole lot of sense. What happened five years ago?

They hadn't given me all the details on the crimes themselves, just the charges. He certainly had been busy the past five years, I would give him that.

I let my mind wander over the matter as I got myself something to drink. Unfortunately, it wandered further than I would have liked when it started going back to the strange detective I had seen at the station. That surprised me. Part of it was curiosity about what case would have led a Hartford detective down here to Adelheid, because it had to be preternatural, but another part of me knew it was because she'd been gorgeous. The thought just seemed to have come out of nowhere, but then, thoughts did that sometimes.

Indulging myself for a few minutes, I went to my computer. The internet being the incredible thing that it is, I simply did a Google search for Samantha Moore Hartford CT PD and waited to see what came up. There wasn't much. A couple profiles on social networking, some Samantha Moores who weren't the one I was looking for. There was one article, however, that caught my attention. It was a little news story from the *Courant*.

It linked Detective Moore to the search for a woman named Anne Rau in connection with a murder.

"Im namen des Vaters..."

The murder part wasn't what shocked me. The name

Anne Rau had me frozen to my seat, however. I knew Anne Rau, I was quite sure of it. I didn't think there would be another. I was after her myself, but before you say that makes three cases I was working instead of two, I'll tell you that Anne was no case to me. It was a personal matter, and one I'd been working on for decades.

Anne Rau, which wasn't the name she was born to, was my sister.

Chapter Five

Although I had started working in the field in the '80s, I had become a *real* hunter the moment I learned that my sister had become an evil bitch. Since that time, I had found her fingerprints on everything from bank heists to drug trafficking. There seemed to be little she wouldn't involve herself in if it suited her, but she had thus far been the one case I couldn't crack.

She was as powerful as me. She was as keen and skilled at hunting and hiding as me. She had the benefit of having even less ethical standards than me, and I would never claim to be a saint.

Moore was looking for my sister, and it had led her to Adelheid. Was it because this was the paranormal 'capital' of the area? Or was it a specific piece of evidence? Could my sister be in the area and I not know it? That was a blow to the senses and the ego alike.

I needed to talk to Moore, but I couldn't just come right out and ask. I would have to go about it very carefully, which meant I couldn't rush it. I would have to consider my approach and work with skill. The shock had brought emotions too close to the surface, so I couldn't do it now. I couldn't even think about it now.

I knew Moore wasn't likely to catch my sister in the next day or so, not if I hadn't gotten her in all these years, so I had time. But she might still have some useful information, so I would need to talk to her.

First, I would have to calm down. I had other work to do, and I could use that to focus. I would work, like I had always done, to distract myself from the wounds too deep to see.

I would work.

I went to the address on file for De Laurentis. Not out of any great hope or feeling that I would find him or anything useful there, since the cops had already been through it with a search warrant, but it was a place to start. Besides, one never knew. Life liked to surprise you, or jerk you around, depending on how you looked at it.

The address was in Infinity Park, which was one of two exclusive gated communities on the outer edge of Adelheid. Typically speaking, the only people who lived in them were very old vampires. Mind, I didn't know of any ancients, but the city had its fair share of the fang crowd past five hundred, which was old enough to have accumulated a lot of money and power. Those that had reached that mark liked to stick together.

There were probably a few humans and shifters living among them, as well, who had more money than they knew what to do with and thought it was a 'dangerous thrill' to live amongst so many old vamps. I thought they were idiots, but to each their own.

Parking down the street, I changed form as soon as I was out of my car. I started off as a dog so I could cover more ground but still be able to blend into the background. Once I was closer to the gate, I turned into a mouse. I'd gotten used to the effects of the shifts and different species years ago, although the height differential could still be a tad disorienting.

In this form, I easily slipped past the guard in his little booth, and the gate was no block at all. Of course, it took a long time for me to get there, but it was worth it.

I skittered along the curb and avoided any obnoxious

hedges that might hinder me, or even the errant thatch of grass. I needed to be out of sight of the guard before I switched into something that could read the numbers on the houses, so I kept in rodent form while curving around the first bend. Infinity Park, appropriately enough, was a road in the shape of the infinity sign, or a narrow sideways figure eight.

Once around the curve, I went back to being a dog. Large enough to see what I needed to see, but not so big as to draw undue attention.

It all helped to get my mind off things I didn't want or need to be thinking about right now. Long ago, I had learned how to narrow my focus when I needed to.

Just before reaching the center junction, I found the house I was looking for. It was huge, suiting this neighborhood, although the style was more modern than one would expect for a vampire of that age. This park had been built nearly a decade ago, by and for vampires, but when we were all still in hiding. Perhaps that explained the modern look.

I slunk around the house, using both the senses of the preternatural and the dog to inhale all scents lingering on the grounds. It was mostly vampire. There was a lot of vampire. You could tell by the faintest trace of death and decay. No human, or even many paranormal species, could even detect it. Those that could usually had to work for it. The scents didn't differentiate very much, however. I could detect subtle differences, but it was just vampire, vampire, and more vampire.

There weren't any sounds coming from within. If he was in there, he was in his daytime coma without any non-vampires in there with him. I peeked in windows without curtains and didn't see anyone. I didn't see any furniture either, but that didn't mean anything. All I saw through one of the windows was a pair of paintings of bearded blond men, one standing in the ocean, and one with a hammer of some kind. It seemed odd, but I was no art critic, and there was nothing else interesting through the downstairs windows. There was a second story. Still, somehow, I didn't get the feeling there was anyone inside, vampire or otherwise.

The longer I was around the house, the more I could discern different scents. I caught onto wisps of human and shifter, but they were few and far between. Then there was another that caught my attention. It was different and familiar but distant. It reminded me of the scent outside my door, yet it wasn't the same person. It was less than the vampire but more than anything else I picked up on, which made it annoying. It was the lingering scent of déjà vu, and it pissed me off.

Deciding this was the bust I had expected it to be, I turned back into a mouse and trotted down the road to the gatehouse. A car sped toward me. I shrieked angrily, but from a mouse, who would know? And then jumped out of the way just in time. I continued shouting an angry little tirade at the car's swiftly retreating rear end, but then went about my business, leaving Infinity and returning to my car.

❪O❫

I had been driving for about five minutes when I noticed a vehicle in my rearview mirror that had been with me through several turns now. It might have been coincidence that someone else was driving the same path I was. There were a lot of people and a lot of places to be going in the city, but the hair on the back of my neck was standing up, telling me this wasn't a coincidence. There was something going on here.

Seeing as how my instincts had kept me alive on more than one occasion, I decided to listen to them. I kept driving until I found a gas station with a moderately busy parking lot, which I pulled into. I parked in front of the store and looked again in my mirror. The strange car pulled to the side of the road, just a little ahead of the store but close enough for me to see. I peered closely and watched as the driver, a man, lifted something to his face. I realized after a moment that he was taking freaking pictures.

That was as much as I needed to see. I hauled myself out of my car and started across the street. I didn't run, because that tended to attract attention, but I walked quickly and with purpose. I had to imagine I looked something like one of those killers in a teenage slasher flick. You know, where the bad guy always walks yet manages to catch the teens as they sprint away? Anyways, I was pretty sure that's what I looked like.

The man in the car appeared to snap a couple more pictures before realizing I was heading directly for him. He stared over the top of the camera for a moment, and then dropped it into the passenger's seat. There was nothing remarkable about him, which I imagined suited his job as a private investigator or general stalker. Eyes and mouth shaped in a silent 'oh shit,' he put his car in gear and sped away before I reached him.

I stared down the road, glaring at his taillights, before realizing I was about to become a statistic in the accident investigations records if I didn't move. Returning to my car, I was very unhappy, to say the very least.

Once behind the wheel, I waited before starting the engine again. I knew it wouldn't be a good idea to drive right away, because I'd be thinking too much about why someone was following me and how I wanted to go find their car and smack them around, perhaps throw their camera on the ground and stomp on it as a horse.

There were people I needed to talk to. To take some steps forward, there were people I needed to talk to. I needed to talk to a really old vampire. I didn't know any ancients, but one over five hundred would do, and I knew at least one that age who might be inclined to give me a little help. It would mean going back to 5, but I could live with that. Though not until after dark since the vamps wouldn't be awake yet.

And then I came back to it. I needed to talk to Detective Moore. I would have liked to have said I wanted to talk to her just because she was so lovely, and I would want to see if she fell on the right side of the spectrum for me, but I wasn't very good at that. And I couldn't say that's why I wanted to talk to her. She might have news about my sister that could help me, and if she did, I needed it.

How was I going to do that? One idea had occurred to me. It was something I'd done in the past, but that was before I knew the cops in my hunting area. Here, I did, and my usual plan could get me in hot water. I wasn't sure I wanted that headache. On the other hand, if I got away with it, this was a detective not from the area so it might have a chance to work and leave me in the clear.

First, I went home. I needed to get myself to the right mental place and also take some notes about my day thus far. I liked to take notes to help me keep track of things. I also had to pull some information off the internet to help in my little scheme.

Once that was done, I went out again and drove to the station. I parked a few streets down and shifted faces as soon as I got out of the car. The face and body I wore were that of an FBI agent who worked out of New London. The entire ploy hoped that Moore wouldn't know this agent because the FBI and local cops didn't usually have cause to work together, or at least not enough that I couldn't bullshit my way through this.

I walked in and flashed my credentials, created through my shifting ability, even though it took a lot of effort, and got in past the front desk. I was directed to the desk where Moore worked, and I was relieved that no one who knew me was around. Not that I thought they would easily see through my guise, it just made my life easier here.

"Detective Moore," I began as I walked up to her. She was even more stunning up close. That was going to be a distraction. She nodded. I showed my credentials. "Agent Ford, from the New London office. I was wondering if I might speak to you about Anne Rau."

Moore's expression was clearly surprised. She looked at my credentials, touching the bottom of the wallet to tilt it up for a better view before nodding. "Of course," she said. Her voice was smooth and cultured. "I don't have an office here, but we can use one of the interrogation rooms." She got to her feet and led me in, shutting the door behind us. "I didn't realize the FBI was interested in the case."

I sat down, looking casual but in command. "We believe that she may be connected to another case of ours, so I wanted to see if you had any information that might assist us."

"All right," she said. "Can I offer you some coffee before we get started?" I shook my head. "I'm just going to grab myself a cup. I'll be right back."

This was going better than expected, which could mean trouble, but I was going to hope for the best.

The lovely detective returned a couple minutes later with a cup of coffee and a folder she laid on the table as she sat across from me. "What can you tell me about your case?"

"Not a great deal, unfortunately," I said with an apologetic smile. It was a thin rope to walk on. I needed to be friendly and helpful enough that she would want to help me, but also secretive enough to be a convincing FBI agent and to cover my own ass. I didn't want to reveal any of my information while trying to get her to tell me plenty of hers. "The name has come up in connection with preternatural and human trafficking in Connecticut and New York."

"When you say her name has come up, can you tell me in what capacity?"

I considered my answer. "As a potential accomplice, though to what extent, I cannot say." That much was the truth. However, I couldn't tell her I knew my sister had been deeply involved in a great many crimes, including the one I was playing up.

Moore smiled. It was a gorgeous smile, but I could see something behind it. I wasn't sure what it was, though, and now I knew her to be a good detective, at least in being unreadable. That wouldn't help me. "Of course not," she said wryly. "What do you want from me then? My case has nothing to do with yours, I'm sure."

"How can you be sure?" I pointed out. "Can you be certain there isn't a connection?"

"I suppose not, but I don't think there is. I've been on this case for several months now and nothing has turned up that would have pointed me in the trafficking direction." She paused and sipped her coffee. "I think something like that would have had a hint by now."

I nodded, like I was conceding her point. She was likely right anyways. "What led you here to Adelheid?"

Moore brushed hair behind her ears, and then settled a hand on the tabletop, resting it over her cell phone. She looked like she was thinking. "Nothing dramatic enough to break the case open." The woman was hedging, choosing her words carefully. "There have been two sightings of her here, so I came to follow up on them and see if I could dig up anything else in the area while I was at it."

"Have the sightings proven to have any truth to them?" I asked, carefully avoiding sounding too eager.

"So far, I'm still following leads." Her phone vibrated. She flipped it open, read whatever was on the small screen, and then closed it again. "After all, I haven't been here very long. I'm surprised you already followed me here, quite frankly." She smiled again, but now I recognized what I saw behind it: she knew something. This wasn't going to go well after all. "So, who the hell are you really?"

I had to try to play it out. I put on my best confused expression. "What do you mean? I have already told you who I am."

She shook her head. "The front desk just texted to let me know that Agent Ford is at her office, in New London, and could take my call, so I'll ask you again. Who the hell are you?"

We stared at each other for a long moment, and then I smiled. "You're very clever. How did you know?"

"I just did," she replied, still being cagey. "I don't know what's going on. I'm guessing you're a fae with some really skilled glamour. Either way, whatever you are and whatever your game is, I'm going to have to arrest you for impersonating an agent of the FBI. Please stand up, turn around, and put your hands behind your back."

"I'm impressed," I said. I did stand up, but that was as far as it went. "You're better than I expected you to be." I smiled darkly, and then leaped for the door. She moved at the same time, but I was faster, and as soon as it was open, I dropped to rodent form and rushed away. No one could see me, and I moved too quickly to be caught. I didn't change into a human form again until I was at my car, and I made a speedy drive home.

How had she known so quickly I wasn't who I claimed to be? Perhaps she knew Agent Ford, or perhaps it was something else. I couldn't say, but I dearly wanted to know. I was impressed with her, like I had said. I wanted to know more, but approaching her at all would only cause suspicion. I only had a slim chance of escaping this coming back at me as it was, I figured. I could hope for a bit of good luck, but that had been in short supply for me lately, hadn't it?

CHAPTER SIX

I waited at home until dark, mulling over what little I had gleaned from Moore about my sister and about Moore herself. My phone never rang, and no one knocked on my door, so I was left to think in peace and by nightfall, I felt I had gotten away with my little stunt. I was frustrated by my lack of success in gathering information but relieved I had escaped judgment.

So, after dark, I felt it safe to go back about my business. Once more, I was forced to push my sister from my mind and focus on the tasks at hand. I decided to start with Carrie and follow up on the tip Myles had given me. I drove downtown and walked into the bar called Phoenix.

This one was vastly different than 5, looking much more like your typical human night club rather than the dark gothic feel of your typical vampire bar. I had trouble picturing Carrie in a place like this. The other seemed to suit her more, but I would follow the lead. I started with the bartender and instantly recognized him for a werewolf.

"Can I help you?" he shouted over the throbbing bass.

"Maybe." I pulled a picture of Carrie from my pocket and showed it to him. "Have you seen this woman?"

He took a moment to thoroughly examine the picture, and then thoroughly examine me. "Are you a cop?" He sounded suspicious.

I shook my head. "No, I'm just looking for her. I'm a friend."

After considering me and my answer during a long pause, he nodded. I wasn't really sure what he was nodding about, but I guessed it meant he accepted my answer and didn't think I was a cop. "I've seen her in here," he said, "just a couple of weeks ago. She was talking to one of our regulars."

"Is this regular here now?" I was hopeful but wondered if my day's luck had run out already.

He stood on his toes and looked around but shook his head. "I don't see her in her usual spots. She might not come in till later. I mean, she's not here, like, every night or anything. I don't know when she'll be back."

The boy was answering my question before I even asked. I wasn't sure if I appreciated it or was annoyed by it. Either way, I left.

I headed back to 5 to talk to Quintus. I didn't worry about whether he'd be there or not, because he was always there. I'm not entirely sure he ever left.

The uncooperative girl was there again and sitting in the same place. She didn't even look in my direction as I came up to the bar. I saw the flash of Quintus's teeth as he smiled at me.

"I didn't expect to see you again so soon," he said.

"I guess I just missed you." I smirked. "I was wondering if you had a minute to talk."

He spread his hands. "We're talking now, aren't we?"

Well, if he wanted to be literal about it… "I meant in private. I need to ask you some questions about being a really freaking old vampire." I smiled in that mirthless, smartass way.

"I'm flattered." He nodded to one of the waiters, who came from the table he was cleaning and took up Quintus's place behind the bar. Quintus led me into a back room, which was decorated in the sort of opulent way you would expect from a vampire, but still with austerity and care. That is to say that it wasn't horrifically gaudy.

He folded his large frame into the sofa and waved my invitation to sit in any of the other chairs or sofas in the room. I took a seat in a chair across from him.

I weighed how much I wanted to tell him. It wasn't precisely a matter of trust, but also that I tried to keep as much of my work to myself as I could. It just felt more professional that way, but you couldn't keep it all. "I'm hunting an ancient." I figured I would say it outright and get that out of the way. "I don't know as much as I'd like about vampires that old."

"There aren't many that do," he replied. If he was surprised by what I said, he didn't show it. "There are not many of them, as far as anyone knows, and most of them hide. I doubt it's because they feel like they have to, but it's become habit after such a long time. You don't get over that in a year. Is there something in particular you wanted to know?"

"'Everything' would probably be a bad answer, right?" I asked. He nodded. "I need to know what sort of power I'm going to be dealing with, and what sort of habits a vampire that age might develop."

He was silent in the way only vampires can be. "Answering that might be the same as if you had asked to know everything," he finally said. "Different vampires age differently, like any other being. Some vampires turn and end up with powers that others don't have. For example, some vampires can call animals. The one thing that remains consistent, as far as I know, is that the older the sire, the more power he or she has over his or her fledglings, even if they're older. Every sire can call their creations and basically force them to come to them, but the elders are even more powerful at it."

The sudden change in Carrie's behavior before she dropped off the map, and the suddenness of said dropping came to mind. I was here to talk about De Laurentis, but this might be information that impacted Carrie's case. Had her sire called her? She never talked about him, so I only knew it was a he and not a she. Why wouldn't she have said anything about it? Maybe that wasn't what happened, but it was as good a theory as any.

"What other sorts of powers can a vampire end up with?" I asked, shifting gears in my thoughts. I had heard vague things about these powers before, but never explicitly.

"I don't know all of them, I think," he said. "There are animal callers, and there are vampires that gave birth to the idea of incubus and succubus, who wield and feed off sexual energy, and there are healers, but they are exceptionally rare. I've heard rumors that some can change into mist, like in *Dracula*, but I've never had any direct knowledge of one so that could be nothing more than a myth."

I certainly hoped it was. I didn't like the idea of that mist thing. The others were intriguing ideas, and I wondered if De Laurentis was able to do any of that.

"Do you know if the older ones have any different hiding habits than the younger ones do? I mean, anything I can use to track my ancient down?"

Quintus shook his head. Briefly, I wondered how that worked when he barely looked like he had a neck. "It depends on the vampire. Contrary to popular belief, we aren't all exactly alike." He smiled wryly. "The more you know about the ancient you are after, the better you'll be able to guess what he or she is likely to do. Vampires often gravitate toward the familiar, like things that remind them of their human lives. And older vampires are often creatures of habit, so if you can learn anything of him from long ago, it very well might still be true today."

This was all good information, although I knew most of it already. Still, it was useful to have it confirmed.

"Is there anything else you can tell me?"

He smiled without joy and shook his head. "Be careful."

I laughed quietly. "That is not something you have to warn me of. I know very well I am walking into a great dark forest with this one."

Quintus tilted his head curiously. He didn't blink. Vampires rarely did. It was kind of creepy, but I wasn't going to admit it out loud. "That's an intriguing analogy, but I suppose an accurate one. I'll simply say you shouldn't run or even walk into this forest. Creep about it and keep an eye out."

"I intend to," I assured him.

❨○❩

Quintus had to get back to work, but he let me keep the room for a few minutes. I admit I allowed myself that time to wallow and sulk over the fact that I'd been talking a lot but little had been said. That didn't last long, however, because I didn't like to linger on it. I wished action above thought, so I left the room.

On my way out, I saw that Carrie's...friend, or whatever she was, remained at the bar, and my usual plan returned to me. I thought that it might work better here than it had on Moore at the station. So, I walked out, but before I reached the door, I paused in an empty moment and shifted to a new face. This was one of my harmless faces, or so I thought. Cute had a way of disarming folk, after all.

I walked back into the bar and affected a look like I was newly-arrived. I glanced around, like I was looking for someone, before taking a seat just a couple of places down from the woman. She glanced up, briefly, before turning back to her drink, which I noticed she was again not drinking. Not that I was surprised. No human could safely stomach too much blood. It wasn't in their nature, any more than it is in the nature of vampires to eat the food they ate in life.

"I hope I'm not going to be stood up." I sighed dramatically, forlornly.

"Meeting someone?" the woman asked. She looked like she didn't want to and yet couldn't help herself. Cute always worked. However, it made me work extra hard to restrain my tongue so I didn't reply to the question's obviousness. If I was afraid of being stood up, of course I was meeting someone.

I flashed a big smile. "I'm hoping to," I agreed. "But you know how these things can be."

She nodded. "Yeah, I do." Pausing, she risked another glance up. "This person already late, or are you worrying early?"

"Only a little late." I forced a casual laugh. "I don't know this Carrie chick too well, though, so I don't know if she's the type to be late or if I should be wondering why I'm here at all, you know?" My casual name-dropping had the desired effect. I saw her flinch, but I went on like I hadn't noticed it. I offered my hand. "My name is Dee Rawley."

"Nice to meet you, Dee," she said, but her manner was stiffer now, even as she tried to hide it. "Rachel McNamara."

Oh, now I had a name. That was promising. At the very least, it was a start, and more than I had before. "Good to meet you," I said. I caught sight of a strange mark on her neck. It looked like a tattoo, but it was little and pale. Like a two-headed arrow cut in half. She turned her head again, and I couldn't see it anymore. "Are you meeting anyone?"

She hesitated before replying, but then shook her head. "No, I'm not." I smelled fear suddenly. That was interesting. It's hard to describe, but someone like me knows it when they smell it. I wondered at its source.

"Do you mind if I sit with you for a while then?" I asked, still putting on a show of being open and friendly.

"Sure." She didn't really sound like she liked the idea,

but I still pretended not to notice these things.

She was human, so she'd have no way of knowing I wasn't exactly what I was pretending to be. It was kind of fun. I put an elbow on the edge of the bar and leaned against it, casually looking around and seeing the outlines of others in the darkness. Most of them were vampires doing whatever creepy-ass things vampires did in places like this. I didn't really want to know the details.

I still wondered how McNamara wasn't swamped. Had Carrie put some sort of mark on her? Carrie had never admitted whether they actually did that or not, but in some situations, one had to suspect.

After a few moments, she got up and pushed away from the bar. "You know, actually, I have to go. Hope your...friend shows up." She bolted without so much as look back.

Grinning, I watched her retreating form. I gave it enough time for her to be well and truly gone before I also left. For no reason I was particularly aware of, I didn't bother to change my face back. This turned out to work in my favor.

As I stepped through the door, I happened to look to my left and saw a man loitering at the corner of the building. That wasn't unusual for a bar, but I also recognized his face. He was young, at least far younger than me, somewhere in his early thirties, I guessed. He had a scruffy face and dark hair, and a camera half-hidden in his hands. It was the bastard I had scared off at the gas station.

This was my opportunity, I thought. He was watching for me and paying no attention to me. I smiled and turned to walk toward him. As I drew closer, he saw me and smiled hesitantly, putting the camera behind his back.

"Hi," I said with my best lash-batting expression. "Looking for someone?"

"No, just...enjoying the night air," he replied uncertainly.

I nodded. "It is nice out, isn't it? I was about to take a

little stroll, clear my head. Do you want to walk with me?"

It was far too direct, but sometimes people fell for that. He, on the other hand, didn't. He eyed me suspiciously instead, and I could read his thoughts all too obviously scrolling through his eyes. He wondered who I was and why I was suddenly interested in him. He wondered if I was a vampire looking for a good vein to open.

"Sorry, but I'm going to stay here, I think," he said, speaking politely just in case I actually was what I appeared to be: a pretty girl taking a shine to him.

"Too bad," I cooed, putting my hand on his chest.

Before he could look down and move my hand, I spun us around the corner and into the shadows of the unlit side of the building. I shoved him against the wall with my hand on his stomach. As I did, my hand became a claw with very sharp nails, and I changed back to my usual face. I saw recognition in his eyes, and then a little anger at himself for not being more guarded.

"Who are you?" I growled. Now was the time to get serious. "I know you've been following me and taking pictures. Who are you working for?"

He didn't reply. I dug my hand a little deeper into his abdomen, and he winced. He felt the tips of the claws at work.

"Do you ever spend time wondering what it might be like to be disemboweled?" I said in a purposefully low tone. "Now might be a good time to start, because that's what is going to happen if you don't tell me what I want to know. Just imagine what will happen when your blood is all over the pavement outside a vampire bar."

I watched his complexion lose all color. "I'm Tim Wilder. I'm a private investigator."

"No shit," I said. "Who are you working for?"

"I'm not going to tell you that."

That surprised me, and I would have to admit it

impressed me, too. It took some balls to say that to someone in the circumstance he was in. It didn't help me any, but it impressed me.

"You do realize your situation, don't you?" I tilted my head and bared my teeth slightly. I had found that, even in human form, humanoid and animal creatures alike reacted to it with the same instinct. "You would do wise to cooperate."

"Look, hunter," he said, finding his steel again, "I don't reveal my clients. You can jab that hand in all you want, I'm not telling you shit. Would you?"

I didn't reply right away. I wanted to give him that long tense silence to see how he would handle it, and if that would ease his ethics. When it didn't, I arched a brow and stepped away. "No," I said, "I wouldn't."

His breath came out in a great gush of relief. "Thank you for not disemboweling me."

Shrugging, I said, "I suppose I'm just not in the mood tonight." Truly, I didn't really aim to ever kill people for little reason, but it was best if people believed otherwise. "Don't suppose this will be true the next time I catch you, and I will catch you. You may be good, but I will always be better." I held up my claw-hand and changed it to a human one, making sure he saw. "Tell your employer that the job is over. I don't want to see you again."

"All right," he said, nodding.

Whether he was lying to me or not, I couldn't be sure. He was probably telling the truth to me right then but could very well change his mind later and think he could outsmart me. It wouldn't be the first time someone had tried, but to date, only one person had ever actually succeeded for any length of time.

I stayed where I was. "Get the hell out of here." I nodded at the parking lot and watched him as he went, got into his car, and drove away. It was only then I felt I could do the same.

CHAPTER SEVEN

I got home without anyone else following me, or if they did, they were far more skilled than I. Since I didn't think the latter was all that likely, I felt fairly secure I had escaped further notice.

Inside the house, I made myself something to eat and sat at the table. I took down notes about what I knew so far. Carrie had once teased me about it actually, that I was something of a dinosaur about some things, but I distrusted computers for certain tasks.

It was my belief, and few can argue against this, that someone could hack into my computer and take my files, but if they were on paper, the person would at least have to rob my apartment in person to get at them. I found that to be an advantage if I was to catch them. I knew nothing about tracking a criminal through cyberspace. I was too much a hands-on kind of girl.

Sadly, my information was a little thin and was half made up of new questions rather than new answers. Like in my De Laurentis notes, I wanted to see if I could learn of any abilities he might have been turned with. For Carrie, I wanted to find more about Rachel McNamara, and for that, I might need the cops. I could do some of it on my own, but if they were feeling charitable, then they could get me more information than I'd have access to alone. However, putting a call into them could be sticky so soon after my encounter with Detective Moore.

I did it anyway. What's life without a little risk? I ended up with a uniform whose name was vaguely familiar, rather than Marlowe or Johnston or Moore. I was perfectly glad for this because he didn't seem to have any animosity toward me, so I wasn't in any trouble at the station, and because I was otherwise known to them, he was willing to help me out. I gave him the name and what little I knew, and he said he'd get back to me.

Admittedly, I felt a little cocky for escaping the tag of my own misdeed, and that helped ease the sting of not finding out who had hired that guy to follow me.

With that, I set about trying to form a plan of action for De Laurentis. Carrie was on hold until I heard back from the PD to see if McNamara was an avenue worth pursuing, but my ancient was still a question mark.

Though vampires that age can often be arrogant, and usually are, they aren't usually stupid, so I didn't believe he was still at Infinity Park. In fact, I had it in mind that he hadn't spent all that much time there in the past few years. I could be wrong, but it seemed too obvious, because it was an address the authorities could connect to him. And if he wasn't bothering to hide his attachment to the crimes, then he wasn't going to make it easy for people to find him. He would like fucking with people's heads, and he couldn't do that if he was simply snapped up at his listed address. No, he wasn't at Infinity Park anymore. I didn't know why I'd gone at all, but there it was.

I opened his file. Those who had been arrested and connected him to their crimes all seemed to be from the coastal area of Connecticut, where it sits against Long Island Sound. If De Laurentis was the creature of habit he was likely to be then I imagined he had been born or had been turned close to the sea. Adelheid itself wasn't far from it, either, so that narrowed my scope to between Adelheid and the coast. Not that it was a small area, but it was still smaller than looking at the United States as a hiding place. The most recent news of him had been in Connecticut, so until I knew otherwise, I'd assume he was still here.

Still trying to think like a vampire of more than a thousand years, I thought I would want to be with my kind. It was why he had chosen to live, for however long it was, at a place like Infinity Park. So, I needed to narrow down locations to cities known for having a solid vampire population. Adelheid was chief among them, but it wasn't the only one between here and the Sound.

Turning to the computer, I opened a map of Connecticut and noted the cities I recognized and connected with the vampire population. Yes, this was the sort of information I kept in my head. It was good to know in my line of work.

There were four possibilities, if De Laurentis held true to my theories on ancients, but Adelheid was still the most likely for both vampires and relation to the coast. The only thing that worked against him was that it was also where people were looking for him the most, yet he hadn't hesitated to flaunt himself before, so why would now be any different?

Where else in Adelheid could I look, however? His arrested accomplices would be little help, and the police had already tried. There were no other known associates. Perhaps I'd have better luck questioning people around Infinity Park because I wasn't a cop. I would try that next.

With that decision made, I shut it down and went to bed. For the first time in a while, I slept without dreaming.

☾O☽

The sound of my cell phone ringing woke me up, again. I considered shooting it. I had a gun. I didn't like to use it when blunt force or an animal form would do, but I had a gun. I could shoot it.

I didn't. I answered with a groggy reply that didn't necessarily sound coherent.

"Dakota?"

It was Marlowe.

"Why the fuck do you people keep waking me up?" I grumbled, flopping onto my back.

"You should be a little nicer to me." Her words were light, but her tone distinctly was not. I knew she was queen of the impassive comment, but this wasn't impassivity. It was something sterner. "No one here is very happy about that little stunt you pulled yesterday."

That woke me up fast. I guess I hadn't gotten away as free as I thought. "How did you know?" I wasn't going to bother making her prove it.

She snorted. "Please, give us a little credit. Who else would pull shit like that and make a shift going out the door? I don't know many wererats."

"You're not planning on arresting me, are you?" I scrubbed my hand through my short hair.

"Unfortunately not," she said, and I thought she sounded genuinely disappointed. "We need you too much, and Moore has agreed to it, so despite your *deserving* to be behind bars, you will remain free."

I waited to see if there was anything else, but she said nothing. "Is that why you called?"

"No, actually, I called because you wanted us to run a check on Rachel McNamara and we have news for you." She paused again. She had to be fucking with me because she wasn't allowed to arrest me. I could understand that. It annoyed me, but I could understand it and couldn't really blame her. "She's dead."

"What was that?" I sat up straight.

"She's dead." Marlowe certainly didn't mince words. "The ME is thinking about three or four this morning."

That was only a few hours after I had seen her. Had she left me and gone straight to her death? I wouldn't have imagined that would affect me, and yet it did on some vague level.

"Well," I began. "That sucks. Thanks for letting me know, I guess."

"There's more."

Oh, that couldn't be good.

"Do I want to know?" I was pretty sure I didn't.

"We believe that McNamara's death is related to the case of Carrie Stone. We know that you are tracking her. Against my objections, Captain Roy is going to let you continue, in conjunction with our investigation."

I suppose the idea of a link to Carrie shouldn't have surprised me, but it did. Had she killed this girl? I didn't want to think it was possible, and yet I couldn't ignore the chance. And what was more, this was magnanimity on the part of the police I certainly wasn't accustomed to but wasn't going to question either.

"Okay." I really wasn't at my most eloquent this early. I also wasn't used to the idea of working with someone else, even at a distance, but I knew the police wouldn't let me run free all over *every* case. "What's next?"

"Get yourself ready to go out. I'll call again. You're being allowed at the scene." She hung up.

I looked at the phone for a moment. "People tell me *I* have bad manners."

Not knowing how much time I had, I got up and took a quick shower and dressed. I ate a hasty breakfast and considered just going down to the station, because I wanted to feel in control again, when there was a knock at the door. Maybe that was them. I went to answer it and was caught by surprise when I saw Detective Samantha Moore standing there.

Opening my mouth, I wanted to say something, and yet nothing came out. She was clearly pissed, even I could see that, but God, it just made her more beautiful. I would not have thought it possible.

"So what, was it like a hazing for the new kid?" she asked. "Pull a cheap stunt, run off, and then not get in trouble for it? I had come here looking for a police station. I didn't realize I'd found a frat house."

"It wasn't personal." Maybe it wasn't the best thing to say, but it wasn't the worst, either, I thought. I felt strangely compelled to keep her from being mad at me, if I could.

She looked unimpressed. "It feels personal to me." Without bothering to ask or be invited, she pushed past me and walked into my apartment.

I shut the door and turned to face her, feeling more undone by this near-stranger's anger than in the sharpness of almost anyone else I knew. Stanton was frequently pissed at me, after all, and it didn't bother me anything like the way this did. My eyes followed her as she turned on me again. I thought she was going to say some more angry things, but she didn't. She folded her arms across her chest and eyed me up and down. I wondered if she found me wanting. I wondered why I cared, but then again, I didn't have to wonder. I could guess.

"I'm waiting," she said abruptly.

"For what?" The question was dumb even as it came out of my mouth, but I couldn't take it back.

The look she gave me said the same thing. "What the hell were you doing?"

I rolled my shoulders. God, I hated being put on the defensive. Moving further into my apartment, I sat on the couch. The move was to give me a moment to get my bearings back and stop being so off guard by this woman standing in my home. "I wanted information about your case," I said. It was honest enough, if only part of the reason.

"You could have just asked." She didn't sit beside me. I hadn't expected her to.

"Not really," I replied. I began to feel like my mental feet were on mental level ground again, so I could get back my usual attitude.

She was waiting again, but I just watched her. Neither of us said anything, waiting to see which one would crack first. It wasn't me.

"Damn, Marlowe was right about you," she said. That wasn't what I'd been expecting, but at this point, I was trying not to guess at much of anything.

"I probably don't want to know what she's said about me." I smiled darkly, feeling more in control of the situation again.

"She said you're infuriating."

That wasn't as bad as I thought. "I've heard that one before."

"I'll bet." Moore stared at me, silent and still angry for a time, although I thought it looked like her annoyance was fading. I knew it couldn't be my wit and demeanor charming her, so she wasn't the type to hold onto anger for long. "You're really not going to tell me, are you?"

"No."

She sighed. "Well, come on then."

I blinked. "What?"

Moore was already heading for the door. "I'm taking you to the McNamara crime scene, so get your ass moving. It's not like I have a great wealth of patience for you right now as it is."

Chapter Eight

Rachel McNamara had lived alone in a tiny house right in the center of town. The lawn was sorely in need of care, and the entire outside looked like a rejected lover still in the wallowing stage: dirty, unkempt, and falling apart.

It was no better once I got inside, either. McNamara had been a slob in life, almost to psychiatric proportions, but the living room was strangely clean. All the furniture was organized against walls, and there was nothing in the center of the room. There wasn't much else, either, as the trash and clutter that decorated the rest of the place wasn't in this room.

Signs of a fight were obvious. The body had been removed already, but the blood remained where it had been spattered on the walls, dripped along the floor, and finally ended in a puddle in the far back corner. I saw an indent in the nearest wall where, I guessed, a body had been thrown with great force.

Moore walked ahead of me and greeted the other officers. Marlowe and Johnston were both there. The former gave me a dirty look while the latter didn't seem to care. Uniformed officers and crime scene technicians went about their business, either ignorant or apathetic about what had passed between me and the detectives.

"What the hell happened here?" I had seen a lot of terrible things in my life, but I hadn't been to many crime scenes. There was something terribly disconcerting, even to me, about the tale of violence written in this room.

Johnston was the one to reply. "Around three-thirty this morning, dispatch received a complaint about the noise coming from this house. One of the neighbors had been woken up and didn't take very kindly to it. Noise complaints aren't particularly high priority, so a car was not immediately dispatched. However, we received another call nearly thirty minutes later and this time, the noise was described as a fight. Someone came to the house, but the noise had stopped by the time they got here."

When he paused, Marlowe continued. "The uniforms walked the perimeter and glanced in the window. When they looked in the living room, they saw the blood and Ms. McNamara's body on the floor. They called it in and entered the house. The back door was open like someone had made a hasty exit, except for a stray dog that was sent away. McNamara was dead when they got there, so they called us and the ME, and here we are."

I tore my eyes away from the red. "What is the connection between this and Carrie?"

"We know what you do," Marlowe said. "Stone is apparently the only person McNamara has socialized at all with in the past few months. We found Carrie Stone's name written down on a notepad on the table with a number. We already tried calling it, and it's been disconnected, but given Ms. Stone's status as a fugitive, and that this scene closely resembles that of the woman Stone is accused of killing, it didn't take a big leap to suppose a connection."

"So, you think Carrie did this?" I asked quietly. The idea she had killed one person was bad enough. I suppose I had always known there was a killer in Carrie, but when it had once been a means of survival, or had been an accident, it didn't feel as bad. The idea that she was getting into fights and tearing people apart hit me harder.

I suppose I didn't keep my expression to myself as much

as I would have liked. I could see in Johnston's face that he caught it but was polite enough to look away. Marlowe didn't notice or didn't care. Moore was the one I caught staring.

"It's our working theory," Johnston agreed after a moment.

They had to know. I must have been listed in Carrie's police file somewhere as a former acquaintance, if nothing else.

I turned away because I had to. I had to find something else to focus on, so I started looking around. Apparently, that's what everyone else did too, because a dull murmur rose up behind me and footsteps started quietly thudding again. I didn't want to know what they thought of me. I told myself that I didn't care, but right at that moment, I did.

Nothing really caught my eye as I looked around. There was just a lot of stuff. I saw various pictures on the wall and books in stacks all over, piles I couldn't identify properly, what looked like movie replica weapons from *Lord of the Rings* in one corner, and just more stuff everywhere else. It all seemed like any other person's home, just more of it, except for the obvious.

"Hey." Marlowe came up beside me. She held a small notebook in her gloved hands. "Rumor has it that you're older than dirt. Maybe you recognize this?" She held it open for me but didn't let me take it. It was perhaps the first time I saw that her scars went past her face.

Ignoring her flattering opener, I looked at the pages. There were strange symbols scrawled from margin to margin. "I don't know it." I shook my head slowly. "It looks like runes, or something like that. Tell your guys to study ancient Germanic or Scandinavian languages."

She nodded. "Thanks."

"Hey." I caught her before she walked away. "Can I have those? I mean, I'd like to look at them some more. See if I recognize anything."

"You can have copies," she granted. "Come with us back to the station and we'll have them made for you."

We both left the living room, heading in different directions, although I knew there wasn't very far to go. I ended up in the bedroom and discovered that a person could develop claustrophobia in a room like this. It was just disgusting. There was laundry heaped in every corner, dishes stacked on the floor with things growing in them, and a rather pervasive smell I didn't want to find the source of. Other smells mingled with it, smells that would have caught my attention if everything else hadn't been so overpowering.

Johnston was in there with me. We looked around for the only free spaces we could find which, for my part, was in front of the dresser. This also had its share of piles of crap I looked over, hoping there wasn't something living in one of them.

It was in between two of these heaps that my attention snagged on something. I peered closer at a knife. It was, in fact, a very old knife with a bone handle. The blade had long ago lost its edge, but it was well kept otherwise. Recognizing it instantly, I reached for it.

"Don't touch anything," Johnston warned sharply.

Wincing, I pulled my hand back. "This is Carrie's." I clenched my fist to keep myself from grabbing the blade. There was a hint of dust and some small items layered around it, so I knew it hadn't been put there that night. "Or rather, it *was* Carrie's."

Johnston came up beside me to see what I was looking at. "How do you know?"

My throat tightened, but I knew I wasn't going to cry. It had been a long time since I had cried over anything. Centuries, perhaps. "Because I gave it to her."

He looked at me but didn't say anything. Instead, he

called a technician over to get the knife and catalog it. We had to step out of the woman's way so she could reach it. As we stepped through the door, he glanced at me. "We might be able to get it back to you."

"I would appreciate that." I didn't return the look.

《O》

Nothing else caught my interest at the scene. What else could compare? I passed the rest of the time in a haze, and everyone seemed to give me a wide berth.

Detective Moore had left at some point, and I rode to the station with Marlowe and Johnston, so I could get those copies. They had a uniformed officer see to that while I sat in the squad room with the two of them. Johnston and I sat in silence, while Marlowe was on the phone with someone. I didn't ask who.

I learned soon enough.

"I just called the ME and talked to Wright," she explained. "He is still working on the autopsy, but he can say preliminarily that the body is torn up. There are wounds all over. She lost a lot of blood, which we already knew because we found most of it at the scene. He hasn't found a bite yet, but it could be hidden by one of the other wounds. He's going to have a full report for us soon and let us know if anything more conclusive shows up."

"I know that vampires don't leave fingerprints, lack of body oils and all that," I began. I still wasn't feeling like myself, but I couldn't just loiter at the edges like a ghost. I had to be involved. "What could they leave? I mean, if Carrie did kill this woman, what evidence could be left behind with the body that could prove it one way or the other?"

Johnston sat behind the desk. "They can leave blood behind, if they are wounded. And a vampire's bite pattern can be just as distinctive as anyone else's, so if we find a bite and can get an image of it, we can make the comparison."

Marlowe chimed in. "It's just trickier with vamps because if they tear while they're at it, they take away much of the impression, and with the fangs, that's easier to do. And there's no saliva."

"Hair is still a possibility. It can still be pulled out, and if we find it, we can test it for DNA."

Apparently, there was more to vampire CSI than I realized. "How long before Wright finishes his stuff?"

Marlowe shrugged. "The autopsy report will take a couple more hours, but we'll have to wait longer for toxicology and DNA, if there's anything to test. We will let you know if it's Stone or not."

I nodded. I needed to know, of course, but that didn't necessarily mean I felt grateful for the information. It would simply be a necessary evil.

The uniform returned and handed me a stack of paper. I shuffled through them, looking at various pages of runic symbols. I saw that someone had made notes in a few of the margins, and it might have been English, but it wasn't very legible. The handwriting was familiar, although it wasn't Carrie's. Maybe I just thought it looked familiar, because I was looking around every corner for a shock or a betrayal.

"You'll be in touch?" I asked them. I didn't see any reason to linger, because all it did was make me think about things I didn't really want to think about. Idly, I wondered where Moore was, but I was probably the last person she wanted to be around.

Johnston nodded. "Sure. And you'll let us know if you find anything new?"

Now, I nodded. "I will."

I left the station and just wanted to go home, find a place to bury myself. I knew I couldn't, but it was what I wanted.

My cell phone rang. I checked the number and saw it was the office. The sun was shining so I knew it wasn't Stanton calling to yell at me about something.

"Hi, Ms. Dakota," Christian, the day secretary, greeted in his cheerful way. "I just wanted to give you a heads up about something. We got a call here at the office. It was someone asking questions about you. The caller ID said it was a private caller, so I don't have a number. I asked her name, but she wouldn't tell me. I didn't answer any of her questions, of course. We entirely respect the privacy of our employees."

It took a lot of willpower to not drive into a lamp post. If it was a woman, then it wasn't the investigator I had caught the other night, unless he had a lackey. I wasn't putting anything past anyone today.

"What kind of questions was she asking?"

"Personal stuff," Christian replied. "She wanted to know where you lived and what your number was. I don't give out addresses and will only give your cell phone number if I can verify the person who is asking."

I wanted to snap at him but restrained myself. I wasn't entirely sure why I did, but I did and wasn't going to analyze it too much. "I know, Christian." I didn't know that anyone had ever told me what his last name was. "I'm not mad at you. You did fine. Just tell me what the fuck this person was asking about me."

There was a long pause. Christian seemed to be a sweet guy, so I'm sure he didn't know what to do with me. I couldn't figure out why he worked for a business like ours in the first place, but I didn't ask these questions. "That was it, mostly. She wanted to know where you lived, what your number was, where she could find you. I pressed for a name or why she was asking, and when I wouldn't tell her anything, she hung up."

"And that was it?"

"That was it."

I sighed. This was getting fucking annoying. It wasn't that I was unaccustomed to people disliking me, but I usually wasn't this popular. "All right, fine. Let me know if I get any more calls like that." We hung up.

By the time I got home, I felt pretty shitty. I still ached inside from the metaphorical sucker punch I'd gotten at the McNamara house and the idea that Carrie wasn't just an accidental killer, but a murderer. How did you reconcile the idea that you had been in love with a murderer? How did one reconcile the idea that more close relations than not were evil?

Inside the apartment, I dropped the stack of papers on the table and threw myself onto the couch. Drained and weary, I fell asleep.

☾O☽

The year is 1628.

I'm standing in my family home with my mother. My brother and one of my younger sisters are with us. The others have gone out with Papa. It is a day like any other, really, although every day is tainted by fear now. Hysteria is sweeping our homeland. Who knows who will be swept under next?

There isn't time for dwelling on things. I try to tell myself that, and that everything will be okay despite what happened in the forest yesterday. I tell myself it was nothing. Nothing will come of it.

They start banging on the door.

"Hexe, hexe, laast sie verbrennan!"

It's a chant that has rung out through our small village more times than we can count, but now it's at our door. Mother gasps. We all know what this means. We have all been waiting for it, and we are prepared. She drops to her knees with a knife and leverages a floorboard up, then ushers us into the cellar, hiding away the knife.

With the floorboard back in place, we wait. Boots stomp above us. Hannah cries softly against our mother's chest, but we all stay silent. We're barely breathing. We're praying they pass us by.

"Im namen des Vaters, des Sohnes, und des Heiligen Geistes," I whisper in my mind.

The floorboard is pried open, and we're forcibly hauled out. We scream, but they don't care. "Hexe! Hexe!" They keep shouting at us as they drag us from the house. Wood smoke drifts thick from the town center. We are being hauled to a waiting hay wagon, but now there is no hay in it. There are people. Papa! Lukas! Hilde! Dagmar! They have already been taken, and now we're going to be loaded in there with them. Are they unconscious? Are they dead? They aren't moving. They aren't fighting back.

I don't want to be burned. I don't want to be burned. I'm not a witch!

We're not evil.

My mother screams as they tie our hands. The humans are awake and are shouting from the wagon, but now everyone is shouting. Everyone is wailing. Only my mother's screams can be heard above the noise as she tears herself from their grasp. We try to fight back, but we are young and scared. Mama moves so fast, I can barely follow as she pulls the knife from her boot and cuts my bonds. They grab and pull her away. She tells us to save ourselves. Tears cover her face as she shifts into a massive bear, swatting away the men like they are nothing.

Mama, no! They are all on her now, pressing her down. Killing her before they even get to the center of town.

I don't want to leave, but I won't let Mama down. I grab the knife, I grab Erik and Hannah, and we run. We run faster than the humans can. We run. We run into the woods. We run *until we are free, and then we become wolves, and we vanish into the wilderness.*

Chapter Nine

I woke up feeling like all the air had been sucked out of my chest. My eyes stung with the memory of acrid smoke, and I coughed until my body caught up, and I realized that it wasn't 1628 anymore, and I was in my apartment in Adelheid.

"Im namen des Vaters..." I pressed the heels of my hands over my eyes and forced my breathing to slow down.

Carrie had given my mother's knife to some human chick. I hadn't asked for the knife back. It had been a gift, a gift from my heart when such gestures were difficult, and what had she done with it? She might as well have given it back by sticking it in my chest. I think it would have hurt less. Now, my mother's knife sat in some cold cardboard evidence box down at the station until God knew when.

I'd come home because I didn't want to be out there anymore, but suddenly my apartment closed in around me like some dirt cellar. Before I started to hear boots above my head, I had to get out.

The sun was starting to set when I got in my car. I drove to Molly's, which was a diner downtown. It served simple food, and I liked that. I also liked that it had an atmosphere that didn't make you feel alienated but didn't actually try to impose sociality on you.

When I walked in, I was surprised to see Moore there. How many times was this woman going to surprise me just by her presence?

I planned to walk past her to get to a booth in the corner and eat alone, but she saw me before I made it. Again, to my surprise, she waved me over. "Have a seat," she said. Her expression made it clear she knew she caught me off guard. I had that feeling of control shifting under my feet.

"Going to yell at me again?" I sat down.

"No." She chuckled. "It didn't seem to do very much good the last time, after all, and I'm not keen to be an example of the definition of insanity." She continued when I frowned. "To do something over and over again, expecting different results?"

"Oh," I said. Who knew? I was crazy after all. "If you aren't going to yell at me, why did you ask me to sit down?"

She took her time, sipped her coffee, and set the cup down before answering. "You're a really strange woman." Moore smiled. "I've heard some interesting things about you, and have learned a few on my own, of course. Quite frankly, you intrigue the hell out of me, although I still haven't forgiven you."

I tilted my head, listening and wondering. "I haven't asked to be forgiven, at least not by you."

Meeting her eyes, I thought she was going to ask who I did ask forgiveness of, but she didn't. Either she thought it would be too personal, or she figured it out. She asked something else instead. "You're hunting Carrie Stone?"

I nodded.

"You knew her before that though, right?"

"I thought I did."

The waitress stopped at our booth. Moore had already ordered, so I put in mine, and the waitress went off again.

"Romantically?" she asked.

I didn't know this woman. I didn't know if I wanted to

know her, although I thought that maybe I did. I didn't know why. It was a feeling. Did I want her to know me, though? So far in my life, that hadn't turned out well. How much did I want to tell her?

"Yes, we were lovers for about a year. It ended a year ago." Apparently, I wanted to tell her that much because the words just sort of came out.

"Is it smart that you're hunting her then? Aren't you a little too close to the matter?" she asked.

I shrugged and slouched into my seat. "I'm not a cop, so objectivity isn't necessarily as important for me. I don't look for evidence that needs to hold up in court. I just have to find people and bring them in. As long as I'm objective enough to not let someone go, then I'm okay."

Not that I thought I was okay at that moment, but that wasn't the point.

She thought about this and nodded. "Makes sense, but I guess I'd still worry if I was chasing down someone I'd been that close to."

"I do worry about it," I admitted, again before I could stop myself. I guess it was easier talking to someone who didn't know me and who I guessed I wouldn't see ever again after her case was done. I still needed that information from her, but I had enough on my plate. "But I also know that if anyone is going to catch her, it's most likely to be me."

"Because you know her best?" she asked.

"Because I'm that good."

Moore leaned back in her seat and eyed me. "Really? You always get the one you're after?"

I opened my mouth to reply, but then felt something. Was she... No, she couldn't be... I felt knocked off the high wire again and closed my mouth. She didn't say anything but just waited patiently for my reply. "Almost always," I finally said. "There's been just one hunt I couldn't capture."

"Anne Rau?" She read my expression. "Yes, I'm that good, too."

"Apparently you are," I said appreciatively. "Yes, she remains the one I've never caught, and I've been trying for a long time."

"Another former lover?"

"No."

"Then who is she?"

I didn't want to tell her. I didn't want anyone to know. It was shameful. "She is my white whale."

Her pale eyes seemed to miss nothing as they watched me. I had the impression of a cat, but I knew she was no shifter. "I'm not sure why, but a Melville reference surprises me from you."

She had a curious way of gliding between topics and leaving me off balance. It was obnoxious, and...alluring. "It shouldn't. I'm not a Melville fan. I just know the same things about the book everyone else does."

Moore laughed. "Fair enough."

"I like the Brönte sisters." I said it. I didn't know why I said it. I mean, it was true, but I didn't know why I wanted her to know or why I thought she might want to know. But I said it anyways.

"*Jane Eyre* or *Wuthering Heights*?" she asked me with a smile.

"Both, but particularly *Jane Eyre*."

Moore nodded. "Now that doesn't surprise me." I wanted to ask why, but she was pushing away her coffee and pulling out her wallet, tossing some cash down on the tabletop. "It's been interesting talking to you. If you don't try to play me for an idiot again, I wouldn't mind getting to know you better." She got to her feet and tossed me a dazzling smile on her way out.

☾O☽

It was dark when I finally left the diner with not one damn clue what to do about the mysterious Detective Moore or any of the other mysteries spinning around me. I decided to go back to Infinity Park. After my previous fruitless venture, it might seem foolish, but I had two purposes. And I needed to be active.

From the file on De Laurentis, I had one photograph. It didn't say where it had been gotten, but it wasn't a police shot. It was candid, like something a person's friend or family might take. Perhaps it came from one of the arrested followers. It didn't matter. I drove up to the gatehouse and rolled my window down.

The guard was a man in his sixties and surprisingly human. Maybe he was a sorcerer, but he wasn't a vampire, and that was the surprise. One would think a human wouldn't want to work at vampire central, but who could tell these things these days?

"Are you on the guest list?" he asked. He knew I didn't live there.

"No, I'm here to talk to you actually." He was surprised. I handed him the picture. "I believe he is, or was, a resident here. Have you seen him recently?"

The guard, whose nametag read H. Daniels, took the picture and gave it a long look. "Oh yes, that's Mr. De Laurentis." He turned his gaze up to me. "Are you a cop?"

I shook my head. "I'm just someone who's looking for him."

His expression was easy to read as he thought about it, and then decided that whatever he was paid wasn't enough to get in trouble if I was lying about being a cop. "I'm sorry to say I haven't seen him in some time. Can't rightly say just how long it's been, but it's been at least a couple of weeks. More, I think." He gave back the picture. Apparently, he had been here more recently than I thought. Being wrong was getting tiring.

"Do you know if he lives alone or if there's anyone staying with him, or in his house?"

"There's been a few folk over the past months," he said. "He hasn't lived here much more than a year, but there's been more in the past couple of months. If there's been anyone during the day, I don't know, but he had quite a few names on the guest list."

I tilted my head. "Can I see that list?"

Daniels shook his head with an apologetic smile. "No, ma'am, not without a warrant."

A girl had to try. "I don't suppose he left anything behind like a forwarding address or a vacation notice, right?"

"No, ma'am. And if he did, I couldn't tell you that either, but he didn't."

"Of course," I sighed and put the photo away. I knew if I asked to go see the house again, he would say no because he was obviously good at his job, so I backed out and parked where I had the last time I'd been here. It was basically a do-over of that night with my entrance taking place the same way until I reached the house.

This time, however, rules be damned, I was breaking and entering. I wanted to see what was inside that house or see if there was anyone in there.

The first step was to take another close look around it and see if there was any sign of a security system. Not all older vampires felt comfortable with a lot of modern technology, but there was always one, and I didn't want to discover too late that De Laurentis had been in that group.

As I slunk around the corner, in dog form, I caught a human scent. It was new and fresh. In fact, it was so fresh that

I walked up behind the man leaving it. Stopping, I realized he was unaware of my presence as he peered through the windows, so I sat down and observed him. He was doing a most thorough survey, although I knew from experience you couldn't see much through the panes.

I followed him as he looked through more windows. It only took a couple more before I got bored and decided to find out what the hell was going on.

Just behind him, I shifted into a human form. As my usual self, I was the same height as he was, so my mouth was right by his ear. "I know what *I'm* doing here…" He jumped damn near three feet in the air as he whirled around. I had my hand at his throat before he could do anything else and had him back against the wall. "So, the question is, what are *you* doing here?"

"I have business with the man who lives here," he said quickly. It was nice to finally find someone who was as afraid of me as they should be. I was finding too damn many hardasses lately. It had done a number on my ego. "I'm just trying to find him, but I don't see anything in there, so I'll just be going, if you'll let me."

"Smells like the truth." I inhaled deeply, leaning my face close to his. It seemed to freak him out more, and I approved. "Just not all of it. What business do you have with the man here?" I paused, searching his eyes. "What's your name?" Maybe it would be easier if I started with an easier question.

He swallowed audibly. "Matthew Thorson."

I released my grip on his throat fractionally as a reward for good behavior. "And what are you doing here?"

Thorson inhaled deeply. "I'm looking for Njord."

That was unexpected. "Say what?"

"I'm looking for the man who lives here," he repeated. My surprise gave him some strength. "I'm looking for Njord."

"Njord… Who the hell is that?"

He hesitated. "Are you going to let me go?"

"When you tell me as much as I want to hear and explain who the hell Njord is." I was getting annoyed, which was dangerous for him.

"I don't know that you'll believe me if I do tell you."

Chapter Ten

My patience snapped. I was tired of being jerked around, and I lifted Matthew Thorson off his feet, sliding him up the siding. "Look," I growled. My voice took on a distinctly inhuman edge. "I am *not* having a very good few days, and I don't have time for your dicking around, so tell me what I want to know or I'll send you through one window and out the other on your head."

He scrabbled at my hand, choking and coughing. "All right!" he wheezed. "I'll tell you!" I lowered him back to the ground but didn't let him go. He gasped, dragging air forcibly into his body. I let him. "My brother is waiting for me in our car. Can we talk there?"

It's not like I had anything to fear, so I consented. "Just don't try anything stupid, like running or pulling a gun. I'm twenty times faster and stronger than you can ever hope to be, and I will not hesitate to use that against you if you piss me off." I let go of his throat. The look in his eyes said he believed me.

I followed him to the back fence. Not having my useful animal forms, he had to hop over it. I flew over and again made him jump a few feet in the air when I touched down with human feet. Once he'd recovered, we walked to a beat-up blue sedan. The man behind the wheel looked a lot like Matthew Thorson, although broader and more rugged. He probably would've had the balls to give me a harder time.

"Who is this?" he asked as I got into the backseat

without being invited.

"She caught me outside Njord's house. She's a lot scarier than she looks, and she wants to know what I was doing here." Thorson had the good taste to appear embarrassed. He looked at me. "This is my brother, Marcus."

"Hi, Marcus," I greeted with a dark smile. "Who is Njord?" I wasn't in the mood to waste any time.

The brothers exchanged a complicated look. I watched them as they did so and briefly wondered if they were twins. If not, they were very close in age. They were also very human, but there was something different about them. As I sat with the two of them together, I could sense the difference, although I didn't know what it was. It was just a sense.

Marcus rubbed the back of his neck, twisting in his seat to face me. "If we tell you what we're doing here, will you tell us why you're here?"

I was right. He was the braver of the two. "Possibly," I conceded. I wasn't going to make any promises.

"And if we don't tell you?"

I stared at him long enough to be unnerving, and then opened my mouth. A little shift in the vocal chords for a very convincing mountain lion shriek sent visible shivers through the both of them. Nothing else needed to be said.

"My brother and I are leaders of...a group of people. Quite simply put, and here's the part where most people stop listening, we believe we are the bodies in which the Norse people and some of their gods have been reincarnated."

"You think you're gods?" I spoke slowly to make sure there wasn't any misunderstanding.

"Reincarnated," Matthew pointed out, like that made all the difference.

I laughed. I couldn't help myself. It was just too ridiculous. I started laughing and didn't stop for a good thirty seconds. Their expressions were unimpressed but not surprised. "Please, do go on," I finally said.

Marcus sighed so heavily I saw his broad shoulders move with it. "When forever died, so did the gods. Ragnarok came and wiped nearly all of them from the face of the land, and those who survived died when people stopped believing in their divinity. But they're gods, and they reincarnated in human bodies, waiting for the day when the major gods— when Odin and Thor and Frigga—would return."

I listened but was already trying to remember the number for Bellevue. "Uh-huh, and who are you guys?"

"Magni and Modi, the sons of Thor," Matthew supplied.

"Thorson, cute. So, Njord is one of these gods, then?" I still wanted to laugh, but at least I could restrain myself now.

"Yes. He joined our group about five years ago. He went through all the trials that new members do, and we were convinced that he was Njord, and the woman with him was Skadi, Njord's wife."

On a lark, I got a picture of Carrie from my pocket. "I don't suppose this is Skadi."

Marcus took the picture and peered at it in the dim light. Shaking his head, he gave it back. "That's not her. Skadi's eyes had more gray to them, and her hair was lighter. I can't say I've ever seen this woman. At least, she's not one of us."

It had been worth a shot. I wasn't believing any of this, of course, but I'd let them keep talking. They might believe it for themselves, and it could be worth my time to play into that delusion.

On a second lark, just to make sure this wasn't a big misunderstanding, I took out the picture of De Laurentis. There was no hesitation when he confirmed it was Njord. At least we were all on the same page.

"So, what's your beef with this guy?" I asked.

"Well, not long after he joined our group, he started talking about how powerful we should all be. He thought we were wasting our time," Marcus explained. "We're kind of a social club. We gather, live communally, study the old texts, make ourselves ready, and work in our community. He thought we were better than everyone else and should act like it. He wanted to be a criminal, basically, and we weren't okay with that."

Those words had a distant echo in my mind that I ignored. "What happened?"

Both brothers sighed. "He fractured the group and took his followers. We remained in Asgard, and he created a new Vanaheim, although, unlike in the past, there is no crossover between the two. We don't even know where he is. We finally learned of this place and thought this was it, but apparently not."

There were a lot of really weird words getting thrown around. I had a feeling that a Google search and Wikipedia hunt were in my future.

"Why bother?" I asked. "If he wants to be a criminal, then let him. He'll get arrested, and so will his followers, and you all can be about your way."

Here, they hesitated and exchanged a look. I waited. "He took something of ours," Matthew finally admitted. "It's an old relic, and it's very important to us. We want it back."

I nodded slowly, thinking about the knife I'd given Carrie. "What was it?"

"Nothing you'd know, I'm sure," Marcus said. "I know you don't believe us, but this is how we live, and this is why we're after him." He paused. "Now, why don't you tell us why you're looking for him?"

"He's a criminal, like you said." There was no harm in telling them what they already knew, after all. "The cops want him, and I'm helping." I decided to let the two of them go without any permanent damage. After all, they had afforded me more amusement than I'd had in a while. "Give me a number. I may want to talk to you again."

Matthew complied and I got out of their car, took to the sky, and returned to mine.

☾○☽

I didn't go home. Instead, I returned to Phoenix to see if the other woman that Carrie had been seen talking to was there. Maybe she would have information, but I knew there was a small part of me that also thought she might be in danger. It would be nice to warn her. Not that I was known for being nice, but I felt compelled. Maybe I felt guilt in some secondhand way.

There was a different bartender this time. I got out the picture. "I'm looking for a woman who frequents this bar, has been seen in the company of this woman?"

She looked over the image and nodded. "Sure, that's Lucy."

This was already a step ahead of my last visit. "Does Lucy have a last name?"

"Fitzwilliam." The bartender didn't hesitate. She was one of the few people to not ask if I was a cop, so while it sounded like she and Fitzwilliam might know one another, she didn't apparently care all that much. "I haven't seen her come in tonight."

One step forward, one step back. "Do you know any way I can reach her?"

The woman smiled. "I do, but I don't think I'm supposed to give out that information."

"What if I told you that she might be associating with a wanted criminal?" I asked.

"I'd say that most of us probably are at one point or another, but I don't want to lose my job." She still didn't ask if I was a cop. The girl was probably smart enough to know that if I was a cop, I would have shown her a badge by now. "I can tell you this much, though, with the hopes that it makes you either buy a drink or leave: she lives in walking distance of here."

I put a ten on the bar and left.

Standing in the street, I made my phone prove it was smart by looking up Lucy Fitzwilliam in the yellow pages. To my amazement, she was listed. There was an address on the same street as Phoenix. It was indeed within walking distance, so I started walking.

When I got to the door, I knocked. It took a couple of minutes, but a woman answered. She was tall and in very good shape. Human. I caught a brief glance of a tattoo on her neck, small and pale. "Lucy Fitzwilliam?" I got a sparing nod as a reply, so I went on, flashing my picture because I didn't have a badge. "Have you seen this woman?"

"No."

"You might want to try actually looking at the picture before you reply." I smirked. "It will make your lie more convincing."

She sighed and looked at the picture. "No."

I laughed. "See, we're already past that point now, because I know you already lied to me once." I loved the ones that made it easy. "Have you seen this woman?"

"What do you want?" Fitzwilliam crossed her arms over her chest and leaned against the door frame.

"I want to find this woman. I thought that was pretty clear by the way I keep asking if you've seen her and the way you keep not answering the question."

"Are you a cop?"

"No."

"Then get off my property." She shut the door.

It was always nice to talk with delightful people. I turned and was about to walk away when I got another surprise.

Carolyn Stone was walking up the driveway.

We stood and stared at each other for what seemed like the longest moment I'd experienced in decades. Seeing her in person turned out to be a bigger punch to my gut than I thought it would be, and the look on her face said the feeling was mutual.

The moment shattered. She turned and ran. I followed.

The winner of this foot race, such as it started out, was not a given. I'm fast, but vampires are incredibly quick. I'd say we were evenly matched when I was still in human form, but I didn't want to shift until the terrain felt less likely to drop me on my face in the middle of it, and I wasn't sure I could take to wing easily here.

She put on all speed because she knew that, at any moment, I would be able to shift and put an end to it. And, in fact, I saw my opening ahead and was getting ready to do just that when, seemingly out of nowhere, an animal raced across my path. Actually, I should say *into* my path because it ran directly into my knees.

We tumbled to the ground, but the animal was gone again so fast that I didn't even know what it was. The scent it left behind was confusing, and the only lasting impression was of fur and unbelievable speed.

My legs screamed in pain as I tried to regain my feet. I fell once but was finally able to get up again, only to see that Carrie was no longer anywhere in sight. Something in me said that the animal encounter was no coincidence. It helped Carrie get away, but what the hell could it have been and how did she get control over something like that? Staring off into the darkened street, I couldn't wrap my thoughts around it.

After coming up with what I thought were some truly ingenious curses, I finally limped back to the home of Ms.

Fitzwilliam but, unsurprisingly, I found no trace of her still in the house. The lights were off, and the door was locked. Yes, I checked. I didn't break into this one. It was quiet again, like any other normal evening, and I'd lost both my witness and my fucking fugitive.

《○》

It was nothing short of a miracle that I made it home. I was, almost literally, seeing red. I was so mad I was certain I had popped blood vessels in my brain or eyes, and it was coloring everything.

My door had just clicked shut when I lost it. I just fucking lost it. I'm not too proud to admit I threw an adult supernatural temper tantrum. I threw things. Furniture. I mostly threw furniture. I shifted into things with claws and tore apart the couch cushions. I took on brute size and pulled a couple of legs off the table and beat the walls with them. Some clothing and cardboard laid aside to be recycled all got demolished.

When I was done, my apartment looked like a tornado had gone through it. A tornado with fur and talons. I sat in the middle of the floor and sighed.

From my pocket, my cell rang. I answered it without looking at the number and heard the voice of my landlord: the elderly Chinese lady who owned the restaurant below my apartment. "What is going on up there?" she demanded with annoyance and concern.

"It would be a little hard to explain." It wasn't hard at all. I just didn't want to. "There will be no more noise now, though."

"Okay." She didn't sound convinced, but she hung up.

I sat like that for a little while. It couldn't have been more than thirty minutes, but it also felt like forever. I eventually started acting my age again and picked up what I could. I was able to screw the legs back onto the table, sort of, but the couch was going to need to be replaced. The walls didn't look any worse than they had before, and the rest was incidental, so not too bad.

When all that was done, I sat on the floor again. I still had an armchair, table chairs, and a bed, but I chose to sit on the floor. I didn't really know why, but I fell asleep there.

☾◯☽

The year is 2010.

I'm lying on my bed. Carrie is there, flat on her stomach, with her chin resting on her hands. She's grinning at me, and light is sparkling in her eyes. "I can't believe it," she says. "You are blushing. Oh, my God. Where is a camera when I need one?" She's laughing at me, but I can't seem to be mad at her.

"All of life is about sex and violence." I'm trying to defend myself and my embarrassment, but I know it's useless. "I'm used to violence. I do it. I talk about it. I'm not used to actually talking about the other, okay?"

"Hey, it's okay by me!" She holds up her hands but is still grinning. "I think I'm rather privileged. I don't imagine almost anyone has ever gotten you to blush, so I take this as some kind of award. It's like winning an Oscar."

I feel more heat flood my cheeks. I hate it. I love it. "I think you're making way too big a deal out of this.

She pushes herself onto her hands and knees and stalks closer. "I don't think I'm making nearly a big enough deal." Leaning forward, she kisses me. "You're like the ultimate hardass, Dakota." She settles back to a seat. "Getting to see a softer side of you is something special, and I'm not going to forget it. Ever."

Laughing softly, I shake my head. I don't want to admit

what a warm feeling her words give me, but my complexion tells on me.

☾○☽

When I woke, my throat was thick with tears that wouldn't come, that never came. I also felt sick to my stomach. The happiness from the dream mingled with my waking knowledge of what had been going on, and the mix was a bad one. I felt like I'd just drunk a gallon of really cheap booze.

Flopping onto my back, I groaned deeply. How could a woman who'd had that effect on me turn so completely around? She had been a happy and loving woman, despite being dead, and now she was a killer. She had run from me. What had she been coming up to Fitzwilliam's house for? Was she going to kill her, too?

Even as I thought it, though, it didn't make sense. Why were these women trusting her and defending her, hiding her, and then getting killed by her? It made shit for sense.

My cell phone rang. It did that a lot. I grabbed it. "Dakota."

"It's Sadie." I sat up, surprised to hear her voice. Truth was, I hadn't thought much about her with all of this going on and, for some reason, it made me feel guilty. "I guess Marlowe doesn't like you very much so she's making me call you. You're being summoned to the morgue."

"Why?" I asked. "I didn't think they had a self-check-in policy."

She snorted. "Funny, but that's not it. Rachel McNamara? Has disappeared."

CHAPTER ELEVEN

I gave it a lot of hard thought during the drive and decided that throwing another tantrum down at the medical examiner's office would probably rope me more trouble than I wanted, so I would have to restrain myself.

"What the fuck is going on?" I all but stomped up to Stanton as she leaned against the wall, arms folded across her chest.

"Hello to you too," she drawled.

I stood and waited. She stood and waited. I was too wound up to wait very long, so I broke first. "Hello," I grunted. "Now, what the fuck is going on?"

She sighed. "It's like I told you on the phone. The body has vanished."

"Don't they have, I don't know, security here?"

"Yes, and specific protocols for suspected vampire victims in case they were given blood."

"And?"

Stanton spread her hands in a what-do-you-want-from-me gesture. "And somebody got past them, although whether it was McNamara getting out or someone coming in to get her is still open for debate. Either way, something didn't work right."

I was twitching. I didn't realize it until I saw Stanton eyeing my foot while it tapped sporadically against the floor. I tried to make it stop, with minimal success. "So, why are you here anyways?"

"A suspected vampire victim vanished. It doesn't look good. The press will have a field day when they hear about it, and I get to try to wrangle them." Her expression showed me just how much she enjoyed that idea.

I forced myself to relax fractionally and leaned next to her against the wall. "Did you know you were actually opening up a PR firm?"

She smirked. I had noticed she did that a lot, even more than I did, and that was probably saying something. "I should have known, and I guess I kind of already got that idea before now. We all do what we can."

"Better you than me."

"You really don't have to tell me that. Put you in charge of PR and we can all go back into hiding right now."

Our sidelong gazes met for a long moment before I snorted, which was close to a laugh, and she smiled. I wasn't going to argue her point, because I couldn't. She was right.

"I take it the cops are here doing their cop thing, and that's why we're waiting in the hallway?" I asked after a moment.

"You would be correct. Marlowe and Vance are talking to the security guard. That Hartford detective is here, too, although I don't know why, really." The mention of Moore was enough to unsettle me, but maybe not in a bad way. "She's asked me some questions about you, actually. Not that I had a lot I could tell her."

I tried to not show my eagerness. "Like what kind of questions?"

Stanton seemed to pick up on it anyway and smiled. "Oh, you know, like what the hell are you and where are you from. Stuff like that. I couldn't tell her that first part in particular since you still haven't told *me*."

That was a slight point of contention between us. In

my time working with the Stanton Agency, I had taken a sort of perverse pleasure in keeping it from her. Now, though, it seemed like that had been silly. "The truth is that I don't know what I am. There isn't some official name for us because my family are the only ones I've ever known. I call myself a theriomorph, after something I read once."

She gaped for a moment, probably wondering who this person was because it wasn't the hunter she'd come to know and be infuriated by. My only excuse was that I wasn't feeling like myself these days. "What all can you really do?"

I shrugged. "I can turn into any animal I have some knowledge of, like have seen enough to emulate, and I can make up different faces and bodies. I don't know what my normal form is because I've been able to shift for as long as I can remember. I don't take the time or inconvenience of other shifters. Otherwise, I am similar with the silver allergy and mostly immune to diseases, super healing and whatnot."

Whatever else we might have said was prevented by the Detectives Three coming out to meet us. Johnston automatically gravitated toward Stanton, and I moved out of his way.

"Did you fill her in?" he asked. Stanton nodded. "We have it narrowed down to a general timeframe of when it could have happened. We're about to go watch the security footage, if you girls would like to tag along."

I wanted to say something about being called a girl, but again I restrained myself. "I'd like to see it," was what I said instead. We all walked down the hall. Moore fell in step with me as I lingered toward the back. My phone rang. I again considered shooting it but answered it instead. It was Myles. "I'll catch up with you." I got a couple nods in reply as they kept walking, and I stopped to talk.

"Any progress?" she asked.

"Yes and no." I considered leaving it at that. "I've got some leads, which I'm presently following up on so I can't talk long." I paused and grimaced. "I almost had her the other night but was tripped up at the finish line, so to speak. I'm still on her trail, though, and I'm this close so I don't think it will be much longer."

"Good." She hesitated. "Are you still handling things okay?"

Oh, not at all. "Yeah, I'm fine. I have to catch up with some people so I'll let you know if anything else comes up." I hung up and hurried to reach everyone else. I found them already in the monitor room, but they were only just getting the images fired up.

Moore was the one operating the computer. I wondered why but didn't ask.

"Someone erased the footage," she said, "for the timeframe we are looking for, but whoever did it didn't know there are automatic back-ups. So, I'm pulling up the video from those, which will just be a moment more..." The television screens came alive, and all eyes shifted from screen to screen, each one showing a different area of the building.

It took a few minutes for anything to draw our attention. I was the first one to catch it, and I pointed. It was the guard desk. De Laurentis walked up and started talking to the woman, but I realized at that point there was no sound. I didn't know what he said, but he was gesturing oddly. After a moment, the look in the guard's eyes showed what he was doing: some kind of hypnotism.

I guess I just learned what abilities he turned with.

We watched on as he walked away. I might have stopped looking then, but he stopped and glanced behind him. A second body emerged on the screen. This time, it was a woman with blonde hair. I saw her from behind and thought maybe it was Carrie, but she turned and I saw the profile. It wasn't Carrie, but I recognized her instantly even before she looked up at the camera, smiled, and crossed herself.

"*Gott in Himmel*," I breathed and rushed out of the room.

It was my sister. My fucking sister was working with De Laurentis, and she knew I was watching.

☾O☽

I ended up in the parking lot before I even realized what direction I'd run in. I started for my car, but the rising tide of panic in my chest overwhelmed me, and I knew I didn't need to drive right then. It might have been my only coherent thought, but at least it was a good one.

"Oh, my God," I repeated a few times. I couldn't stop moving. I took two steps in one direction and then took the same steps back, only to step twice in another direction. I ran my hands into my hair, gripping it until I thought I might pull it out.

Hannah, Hannah, what are you doing now?

I knew that my sister was a criminal. I had been hunting her since the '90s, when I first learned of her misdeeds. We all had to pay for our sins. It was my duty as the oldest to take care of my siblings. As she was the only one I had left, it was my job to take care of her. What 'take care of' meant had just happened to shift from one thing to another.

It should not have surprised me to see her involved in some illegal enterprise, and yet it did. Seeing her on that tape like that was still another sucker punch. And I knew there was only one person she looked at when she looked in that camera and crossed herself.

Me.

"Dakota?" It was Stanton's voice.

I turned to face her and realized it was both her and Moore. I felt cornered, but their expressions were those of comfort. Well, Stanton's was. I couldn't read Moore. I tried to take something away from the fact they were standing there, but the emotion was still running too high in my head.

"Dakota, what's going on?" Stanton asked.

"I know the woman," I admitted with a weak smile. I still couldn't stop moving. I had all this energy electrifying every cell in my body, and yet I had nowhere to go with it. "I know the woman. I had no idea she was involved."

My attention was splintered, which meant entirely useless. I looked at Stanton and was barely aware of the fact that Moore had moved. She was behind me and put her hands on my arms. It was a gentle touch but startled the hell out of me. I jerked. It was like a spasm in every muscle, but her grip tightened just enough to keep me still.

I looked over my shoulder and met her eyes. They were still unreadable to me, but there was something there. Something I wanted to know but couldn't name. Something that helped me calm down.

"It's the woman you're after," I told Moore.

"I know," she said. One hand dropped away from my arm while the other lingered. "We have a picture of Anne Rau."

I laughed weakly. "She's got some gall, I'll give her that," I said. I didn't tell them the half of it either. "Rau was the name we took and lived with for our childhood. I can't believe she's still using it, after everything that's happened, everything she's done."

Recognition came into her eyes. "It's your sister," she said.

"Yeah." I nodded. "It's my sister. She is my sister. You're hunting a woman that's nearly four hundred years old and can wear any face she wants. I've been hunting her for almost twenty years, and I haven't caught her yet."

She removed her hand, but it was a slow gesture that slid it down my arm until separating. "Maybe it's time you started working with someone."

"You really don't have to do everything alone." Now it was Stanton talking, and I turned my head to look at her. I was caught between the two of them but strangely lacked any desire to get away. "Didn't I tell you that when you came to work with us?"

"I suppose you did," I conceded. My heartbeat had finally begun to slow, and my breathing was less ragged. I was grateful to them both for that, but I didn't know how one expressed it. So, I didn't say anything, but I hoped they knew.

There was silence between us for a few moments. "Can you handle this?" Stanton asked. "You're going to be running two hunts with ties to your past. Very emotional ties to your past. I think some people would be worried you might not be able to handle it."

In the past, I would have answered right away and firmly declared that I could handle it, because nothing shook me. I might have believed it then, too, but I wasn't so sure about that anymore, so I didn't reply right away. I stared into her eyes as she stared back. She was so still in that way that vampires were. It reminded me of Carrie, which was the last thing I needed to be reminded of.

Could I handle it? All of my hunts knew I was after them, including my sister. Of course she knew. That was why it was so hard. Would this be biting off more than I could chew? I wasn't sure, and maybe that was a good thing, or maybe not. But I made myself take the time to think about it, even if in the end the answer was the same. Well, it wasn't exactly the same.

"I have to handle it. I have to catch them both and bring them in myself, or I don't know that I'll know who I am anymore. I *can* handle it. I *will*." Was I overemphasizing to convince them or myself? Probably both.

"All right," Stanton said, "but don't go it all alone."

I nodded. "I won't." Pause. "Can I go home now? You all don't need me for anything here, do you?"

Stanton and Moore exchanged a look. "We will need to talk to you more about your sister," Moore said, "but you can go for now."

I swallowed hard, nodded, and headed to my car. At least now I could drive home.

CHAPTER TWELVE

This changed everything, and it changed nothing.

I had to think it through like any other case.

My sister was in league with De Laurentis. To what purpose? He was powerful. She was drawn to power. Now the echo of her words when I had listened to the Thorsons talk about De Laurentis seemed all the more striking. Once the two had found each other, it was inevitable they would connect. Hannah had long thought we were too powerful to live in the human world, and that their laws and morals should not apply to us. The ancient felt the same.

She had to be Skadi. There was no other possibility.

How had they fallen in line with the Thorsons, though? What scheme had come upon them to try to take over some crackpot group of people who thought they were reincarnated gods? I admit, I could see the logic in scamming the crazy, but how had they found this particular group of crazy people and then convinced them they were meant to be a part of them?

On a whim and desperate to be doing something, I opened a Google search tab on my computer and searched for *reincarnated Norse god groups*. Unbelievably, I got a hit on a website that had the Thorsons on it. Look at that, the crazy people had a website.

I started reading.

Surprisingly, the more I read, the less crazy they

seemed. Don't get me wrong, I still thought they were all nuts, but it seemed like harmless crazy on the part of the Thorsons. Their site read like any other social group. Hell, it was all about as innocuous as a book club and read about the same, too.

There were pages on Norse mythology, talking about the gods and who did what and was married to whom and had what power. That all read more like a soap opera, but so did most studies on ancient mythologies.

It was innocently boring enough that it might have placated me after my shock, but it did leave me with problems. On the one hand, I saw how it could be twisted into something dangerous, like they said De Laurentis had. But what could he have taken of theirs that they wanted back so badly? Whatever they believed about reincarnation, they were still human and yet they were chasing down an ancient for it. It had to be something very important.

Nothing I saw on the website told me what it was, however. As I saw it, there was only one way to get the information I needed, and that was from the Thorson brothers. That particular hunt would be exceptionally easy, because there was an address on the website. I also had their phone number, but I liked showing up on their doorstep better.

I left the apartment without a second thought and went there. It turned out to be a massive house just outside of Adelheid. It was in the Victorian style, large. There was a light on outside the front door and inside a downstairs window. I saw a body moving behind the curtains and thought it could have the shape of Marcus Thorson.

Walking up to the door, I knocked. I just barely restrained myself from outright pounding, and it was, indeed, Marcus Thorson who answered the door with quite the look of surprise.

"Your address is on your website, don't look so shocked.

You were not that hard to find." I brushed past him without being invited. We turned to face each other.

"What the hell are you doing here?" he asked.

I inhaled deeply and folded my arms over my chest. "There's some shit you're not telling me about all this, and it just got a lot deeper for me. I need to know what you know and why De Laurentis is so important to you."

He stared openly. "Is there some way I can get rid of you?"

"Not really, no. Except by telling me what I want to know and not lying to me. Believe me, you will not like me when I'm angry." Okay, I cursed myself for the pop culture reference once the words were out of my mouth. Admittedly, I could be big and green if I wanted, but I didn't think it would make me very convincing or intimidating.

He didn't seem to catch it, so that was good, at least. "I don't like people who appear at my door and make demands. We don't owe you anything."

Did people just want to make my life difficult? "And I don't like people that get in my way. This all means more to me than you could possibly know, and I can't get the answers I want with you dead, so please don't make me kill you."

It was obvious he had a far steelier constitution than his brother, yet he did pale a little. He seemed to sense just how serious I was. Would I have actually killed him? It wasn't likely. I didn't like leaving a trail of bodies, really.

Thorson sighed heavily. "I don't see how it's any of your business." He still wasn't ready to let it go and just do what I was telling him to.

"It is very much my damn business, and I can't do what needs doing until you tell me what you know," I growled. The idea of tearing him apart limb by limb was very appealing, but it wouldn't help him to speak, I knew. I forced myself to take a breath. "The sooner that you tell me, the sooner I will be out of here. I don't want to be here any more than you want me here."

Relenting, he gestured me into what looked like a study. We sat down. "It's Mjolnir...and the Valkyries."

"And if you repeated that in English?" Both sounded familiar from the website, but I hadn't committed the details of the mythos to memory.

"Try to keep up," he said. Was this how I came across to people, I wondered. Not that I planned to change my attitude, but I was curious. "Thor, the Norse god of thunder, bore the mighty weapon, Mjolnir, which is a hammer of great power. As his sons, we have the hammer and keep it until his return." He paused. "Or we *did* have it."

I nodded slowly. "De Laurentis took it when he left?" He nodded. "What does the hammer do? Why is it such a problem that he has it?" I didn't believe it had any god-like powers, of course.

His expression changed from one of frustration to one of embarrassment. "We don't actually know."

Setting my elbow on the armrest, I put my head on my hand and sighed. "Really?"

"Really," he admitted. "We have these ancient texts passed down secretly through the years of our order, and for the first time in generations, we had the necessary items to forge the weapon, and no one can deny that it has power to it. I don't know if you noticed, but it's summer, and yet all the plants outside our house are dead. It's because Mjolnir isn't here any longer, like the house mourns its loss. It has power, no doubt. Thor was the god of thunder, so it must relate to that. It's just that neither my brother nor myself can wield it. We can pick it up, move it around, but not use any of its powers."

"If you can't, then why would De Laurentis be able to?" I didn't mention I hadn't noticed the lack of greenery.

He shook his head. "We are not certain that he can, but at the same time, we cannot take the risk." He paused. "There are also the Valkyries."

This sounded familiar. "Something about dead people?" I knew I sounded like quite the scholar. "The name Valhalla coming to mind."

"Right." Marcus sounded like a bored schoolteacher. "The king of the gods had female warriors that would go to Earth and pick the best and bravest of earthbound soldiers, who would then be taken to the king's hall, called Valhalla, where they would live and feast forever in honor. And they would do his bidding in choosing the winners of battles."

"Okay, so what does that have to do with you guys? I can't imagine you all managing to pluck warrior's spirits from anyone."

"No." He still didn't seem very impressed with my attitude. "But none of us choose who we are reborn as. Some are born with the spirits of the Valkyries. They are their own... subgroup, you could call them, of our order. They prepare themselves for when the old gods return, like the rest of us. They train as warriors, though their fighting prowess is never needed outside of training. They tend to pursue jobs like fighting, such as martial arts or gyms or sports."

"Do you have, like, a chart or something with this on it?" I sighed. "What about the Valkyries and De Laurentis then?"

"The woman Njord came with," he went on, grudgingly, and the reference to Skadi was enough to make me stiffen up again, "was very...ambitious. Powerful. Ruthless. She had his attitude, and she liked the Valkyries. She thought they could be a very powerful force if directed properly and took control of them. I don't know how she did it, but she did. It wasn't long after that Njord and Skadi split, taking part of our group with them and all the Valkyries. Only the old gods know what they're doing with fierce women like that."

I sighed. "I have a good idea."

☾O☽

After I left the Thorson house, I had more information but little that helped. I knew he was glad to see me go. I needed to clear my head.

I drove off but didn't go very far. I parked at the nearest forest and got out. It didn't matter to me if anyone could see. I had to get out of this body. I shifted into my favorite form, the mountain lion. It was big enough to still feel powerful, but not as awkwardly large as, say, a Siberian tiger. It suited most purposes, and now it was good to run in. To let go of my human self for a while and simply be the beast.

My mind was the same, but the change in my body and goal seemed enough to convince my mind to let things go for a while. And with any luck, things would remain clearer after I stopped running and returned to human form.

I'm not sure how long I ran. One doesn't have much sense of time when like that, which I guess is part of why I like it so much.

After a while, I forced myself to turn back. With so much on my mind, it would have been easy to lose myself in the primal, but I knew I couldn't let that happen. I went back to my car and drove home. Sadly, my hopes were not fulfilled, and my mind was just as foggy after the run as it had been before.

What didn't help was to come home and find Samantha Moore sitting on the bottom step.

"What are you doing here?" I asked, suddenly wary. I looked around but didn't see any sign of Marlowe or Johnston.

"I have a confession."

My brows rose. "I thought this kind of thing usually went the other way around."

She smiled a little. "Have anything to confess to me?" I

shook my head. "Then shut up and listen." She paused. "I'm a little more than human. Pick what term you want, but I've got a power known as psychometry."

I wasn't particularly knowledgeable on human powers, as I had never bothered to ask, but those I'd known were animators or summoners. I didn't know what psychometry was, but it surprised me to learn it about her. "And what does that mean?"

"I can pick up images, feelings, from objects. It's like I can sort of read the history of that object and learn a little about the person that had it last," she explained. I still couldn't figure out why she was telling me this. It sounded really useful, but I didn't know what it had to do with me. "I am not that strong in it, though. So, it's not the slam-dunk skill for a cop as you might think."

"Okay." I nodded slowly. "Why are you telling me this?"

She smiled apologetically. "Outside the ME's office, I touched your jacket."

I remembered when she'd done that, but it had hardly been inappropriate, so why... Oh, wait. After a moment, it dawned on me. That's when I started worrying, but then she had said she wasn't very strong in her skill, right?

"What did you learn?" I could hear the tightness in my voice, caution and wariness. I stuffed my hands in my pockets because I didn't know what else to do with them suddenly.

"Not much," she assured me, although I wasn't sure if I believed her. "I didn't mean to read you or anything. It just kind of happened. It does that sometimes. I just got some flashes of emotions without any events that would explain them."

That sounded bad enough, but not as bad as it could be. "What did you learn?" I asked again.

Moore sighed deeply. "That you're very sad." She shrugged and still looked apologetic. "And feel very betrayed.

I guess both are understandable, given what little I know." She paused. "And I think I know now why you like *Jane Eyre*."

"It's a really good story?" I honestly wasn't being coy. I was that dense.

"It's about a girl with no family, or what little family she has is dead or turns her out, and she lives a hard life but never forgets her sense of self. She suffers betrayals and hardships until finally getting her happy ending." She smiled a little. "Looking for your happy ending?"

I didn't want to think about what she said, or that it was her saying it. "You're kind of a disturbing woman," was what I said instead. "Do you want to come in?" I didn't know what made me ask, but I asked anyway. Maybe I thought her coming here to confess was a nice gesture I wanted to return.

She looked about as surprised at my offer as I was but smiled and nodded. "Sure, that would be nice." She got to her feet. "I'm glad you're not mad at me. I really didn't mean to."

I shrugged, moving up the stairs. I didn't want to think about it.

I didn't know if she was going to try to pursue it, but when we reached my door, I immediately saw that the lock had been broken. The door was still open slightly. There was a strange scent lingering. I hissed. I sure as hell didn't need the fae wards to tell me someone had broken in by brute force.

Moore was beside me. She had her gun out and nodded sharply for me to step back. I wanted to argue the point because it was my damned apartment, but in a rare occasion, I let her do what cops did. Going ahead of me, I watched her check the apartment, but as it was practically one big room, it didn't take long.

She walked back out to me with her cell phone in hand. Without saying anything more, she was already calling it in.

Normally, that would have pissed me off. Right then, it

didn't. She looked in my eyes as she talked to dispatch. Not just looking but staring into me so hard I began to fear she had learned more than she admitted.

"They're sending someone," she said as she put the phone in her pocket. "Do you have any idea what someone would be after?"

"Well, I certainly don't have any riches in there." I rolled my eyes. "It has to be related to a case, but all my notes are on paper, and they were in my car. So, they wouldn't have gotten anything. Can I take a look and see if anything is missing?"

She nodded. "Just be careful. The officer will want to see things as they are."

More people rifling through my home. That sounded great. "Right." I walked in. Instantly, I saw that my laptop was missing, and I said as much. "I don't save anything on the computer, so it's just a loss of five hundred bucks for a new one."

I looked some more. With every step, glance, and moment, I felt more and more angry and violated. The threads of my life were being plucked at one by one, each one made to tremble and shifted out of alignment. Home was supposed to be a refuge, for anyone, but it seemed it never would be for me. What was I supposed to do about this?

It had been a long time since I had felt so...helpless.

Chapter Thirteen

Moore stayed and helped the uniformed officers do their thing, but there wasn't much to look at. It was obvious the place had been rifled through, but it wasn't totally tossed, and as far as I could tell, nothing else had been taken. They wrote their report, apologized, and left.

She helped me as I cleaned up.

"You don't have to do that," I told her.

"I don't mind." She shrugged. "I would feel kind of bad just leaving it all here like this and you alone. Besides, it's not like I've got anywhere to be."

I thought about arguing, or just bodily picking her up and putting her outside on the step, but I oddly liked having her around. I didn't know what else to say, though, so we straightened up in silence. It was easy to do. My place wasn't complicated, so she didn't have to ask where things went. For a moment, I kind of panicked about what sort of things she'd be reading off my stuff, but I didn't think it would be any worse than it already was.

The silence began to bother me. It usually didn't, but it did then. I stopped what I was doing and straightened up.

"Do you want something to drink?" I asked.

She laughed like she had been waiting for me to say it. "You know what? I really would."

I went to the cabinet and got out a bottle. It would have really pissed me off if whoever had broken into my place had taken this. It was hard to find. The brand was one made by werewolves, and it had been an underground purchase kind of a thing until Cameron's Law, and now you could find it at the liquor store, but it was expensive. It was kind of whiskey, but was its own drink, too. It was much harder liquor than most human drinks.

Showing it to her, I asked, "Can you handle it?"

She walked up and eyed it, smiling uncertainly. "I can try."

"Someone who admits weakness—" I grabbed two glasses and poured. "—I can appreciate that. I'm not one of them, but I can appreciate it when I see it."

"You never admit weakness?" Moore lifted the glass, eyeing the dark amber liquid like a snake about to bite her. "Is that because you don't have any or just won't admit it?" She damn well already knew the answer to that, but I got the impression she was teasing me.

I snorted. "If I said the former, would you believe me?" My glass was half-full, and I drank it in one swallow. It burned like I had just drunk the ninth circle of Hell. I coughed and smacked my open palm on the countertop. My eyes watered. "Damn good stuff."

With each passing moment, she looked less convinced in the drink. "I wouldn't believe you, no." She still hadn't taken a sip. "Because no one is without some weakness."

"I suppose." My concession came with a slightly hoarse voice, but I was already pouring myself a second glass. She eyed me like I was a crazy person. Maybe I was. "I don't like to admit it, then."

"Why not?" She hooked a stool with her foot and pulled it close, sitting down. "If no one is without weakness, then it's no shame to admit that you have some."

I downed the second glass. The coughing was harsher this time. "If everyone is with weakness," I countered, gasping, "then why admit it? Everyone already knows."

Moore smiled. It lit her entire face. Her gray-green eyes literally glittered. There were gems in her eyes when she smiled. "Fair enough," she said, lifting the glass in a silent toast, and then drinking.

It took a moment to hit her. Those eyes watered, and she coughed. She laughed when she did it, which probably made it worse, but her expression was still beautiful, even as she cursed up a storm. "Jesus," she spluttered and giggled, "who the hell makes shit like this?"

I grinned. "Crazy-ass werewolves."

She put her hand on her chest as she gasped for air, and then wiped her eyes with her other hand. I wondered why she did the first. Was she trying to hold herself together? I couldn't imagine it helped her breathe any. "And here I thought moonshine was bad."

Almost gesturing to the couch, I remembered it had no cushions—which she had kindly not asked about—and hopped onto the counter instead. "You've had moonshine?"

"Once." She nodded. "And I thought that was a horrific alcoholic experience, but it doesn't hold a candle to this." The hand moved from her chest to her head. "Can you get drunk off one glass?"

"Maybe humans can," I replied. "I don't really know. I've never drunk this with a human before."

She laughed and pushed the glass away. "Thanks for the warning. I better not have any more. I'm still going to need to drive home."

It was strange, but the thought of her leaving made me sad. I was probably just rattled by everything, but for the first time in more than a year, I felt lonely enough to actually want the company. We all saw where that got me last time. I was chasing my ex down in the streets of Adelheid for murder. So, the desire for her to stay was almost enough to make me tell her to leave, but I didn't. Her ability should have been enough to make me walk her to the door, but it wasn't.

I realized, after I hadn't said anything for a moment, that she was watching me.

"Sorry," I mumbled. The word tasted odd. Probably because I didn't usually say it. "I guess I'm not all here."

"Too much of that would put you on Mars, I think. I'd say Pluto, but I hear it's not a planet anymore." She smiled.

She seemed less affected by the booze than I thought she'd be. For a human, she had a pretty strong constitution. I was suitably impressed. I chuckled. "There is that, though I don't guess it would have to be a planet for me to land on it." The humor faded as a thought, rather abruptly at that, crept into my head. "Do you do much with evidence?"

Moore blinked and didn't answer right away. She was probably surprised at the sudden change of topic, but so was I. "Sometimes," she finally said. "Why?"

I stared at the faux marble counter. "Did you do anything with the knife they found at the McNamara house?" I couldn't get myself to say anything more than that.

"Yes." She nodded. "But I didn't get anything from it. There was too much. It overwhelmed me to the point I couldn't pick anything out. It would take someone with much stronger abilities than me to do it."

"It is a very old knife." My voice was low, half-relief and half-disappointment. I was relieved she didn't know even more about me, but I could have had more information if she had seen something.

She wanted to ask. I could tell by the look in her eye when I finally lifted my head. There was a small part of me that wanted to tell her the things I hadn't told anyone, even Carrie, but I wouldn't ever say it. I couldn't.

Somehow, she knew and smiled. Why did she smile? "I should be going." She got to her feet. "We'll talk again tomorrow. I think there are some things we should probably cover now that our cases are aligned."

It was nice of her to not bring up how I'd known they'd been aligned all along. In fact, she was being impossibly nice to me. I wanted to tell her not to leave but instead, I hopped off the counter and walked her to the door.

She grabbed the handle but stopped and turned. It was then I realized I was frighteningly close. She didn't wear perfume, but I could smell all the other scents that made up her as a person. It was yet another sense she was beautiful to, and feeling as I was, I was overwhelmed.

The moment felt like a movie where the hero and heroine are standing too close, staring at one another's lips with open mouths, unable to move forward or back, and barely able to breathe for the intensity between them. It felt just like that.

The moment broke when she broke it. "Tomorrow," she said. I thought I heard a new edge to her voice and was relieved that it wasn't just me, even if I was surprised by what I felt, and bereft of her presence when she got out the door.

I stood there for a while, hoping to keep her scent in my head but eventually, I had to move.

Oh, hell, I couldn't afford this.

I had two different professional cases intermingling and joining forces with my life's pursuit of my evil sister, while someone was stalking me and that someone, or worse, someone else had broken into my place. I couldn't afford to be swooning over anyone, no matter how beautiful and surprisingly understanding they were.

Grabbing the bottle of liquor, I went to bed and drank till I passed out.

☾ O ☽

The year is 1883.

I'm standing in the streets of London, and I'm staring down a crowded street at a woman in a fine dress. There are a lot of women in fine dresses, but this one is special. Her hair is brown now, and she has it tied up and stuck under a hat, looking like all the other women who pass by. She looks like all the human women. Who among them could possibly guess she is so much more?

She is looking at a vendor's cart. I can't see what it is.

I've emulated my clothing and hair to match everyone else's, because I don't want to stand out. I need to blend in, so I can get to her. That's the only reason I'm here. Why else would I be in this city with its teeming crowds congesting every minute space until you couldn't breathe but for finding another person in your way. How could Hannah stand it? Living as we had been was hard, but at least you could breathe, and you could run if you had to.

She sees me. She doesn't look happy in that first instant, but then she smiles and leaves the vendor behind to come meet me.

We don't hug. Her hat looks silly, and she's carrying a parasol when it doesn't even hint of foul weather. "Anneliese," she says. Now there is warmth in her expression and her tone, but I don't know if I can believe it. "What are you doing here? I didn't think you liked town."

Town? She sounds like one of them already. "I wanted to see you before I left. I'm leaving the area soon. I wanted to say good-bye."

Frowning, she tilts her head. "Where are you going?"

I shrug. "I don't know yet. I just don't like it here, and I want to move on. Maybe I'll go to America. I have seen word of it in the papers."

"It's not the society that London is," she points out. Her laugh is condescending, so is her next reply. "But then, perhaps

that will suit you."

"What's happened to you?" I have to know. Has being among humans changed her so much, so quickly?

She waves dismissively. "Nothing, I've just rejoined the ranks of humanity and enjoy the of others now." She hears something I don't notice and turns her head. I look in that direction and see a brief glimpse of a man. I can't quite make him out, just a short impression. She fiddles with a little trinket hanging on a necklace. It's one of those pieces of jewelry with a white human profile on it. I've seen them on others, but I don't know what they're called.

"I have to go," she tells me. "But good luck. I hope that you find America suiting for you."

Turning, she leaves me. I want to call after her, but I know it won't do any good because she has already dismissed me from her mind. I don't know how, but she has.

Apparently, her sister has become too beastly for her.

CHAPTER FOURTEEN

The first thing I did after waking was to throw up in the trash can next to my bed. The alcohol had left its mark, and the entire world felt like it was wrapped in wool. I had the absolute worst taste in my mouth, too, and that was before the vomit.

Staggering into the bathroom, I rinsed my mouth out for about five minutes, and then brushed my teeth twice. I took a ridiculously hot shower until some of the fabric in my brain began to unravel and I felt like I might be a living being again.

No breakfast that morning. I just sat at the table with my forehead pressed against the wood, waiting for the hastily repaired table legs to break and drop my sorry ass on the floor. So far so good, though.

I thought about my dream. I never dreamed like other people. Memories haunted me instead. Last night's was particularly painful, because there was a very important detail shining like a light right in my hung-over face: the man my sister went off with. I hadn't known him then, and barely remembered him, but now, in my dream, I saw enough of his features to recognize him as De Laurentis.

My sister had been with him for more than a century, and I never had a clue.

Admittedly, he was nearly an ancient then, and they're good at hiding. And Hannah and I were pros at it, too. We'd had to be. But I had to wonder if he'd somehow had something to do with her leaving me. The fact that his words to the Thorson brothers sounded like her words to me when she left became less of a coincidence. Had she met him somehow when we were still living as wolves in the forest, and he'd talked her into returning to the human realm? I would guess to embark on a life of crime, because why should human laws have any bearing on ones as powerful as they?

If I wasn't so damn sick already, it would have made me ill. How could I never have known this was in her, until it was too late? She was my baby sister.

I made it to the sink in time to throw up again.

This wasn't getting me anywhere. It was a moment where I might have sworn off alcohol forever, but I knew that wasn't going to happen, so I didn't even bother to think it. Back into the bathroom for more rinsing and brushing, because it was not a taste I could tolerate for a moment longer than I had to. I'd be brushing my teeth all day if this kept up, and that did not sound like any kind of fun.

I had to think clearly. This had all come together when I was at the morgue because the body of the woman Carrie was most recently accused of killing had vanished. The security tape had been erased, and what was erased was De Laurentis and my sister going in at the time the body had disappeared. And yet Hannah had suspected we'd see it anyway. That *I'd* see it. So, it was clear they did it. And if Carrie was the one who killed McNamara, and I was ready to believe anything at this point, then Carrie was tied to De Laurentis and Hannah.

So, the question was why...and how. So, there were two questions.

Knowing what I did about vampires, the only thing that came to mind was that De Laurentis was Carrie's sire. I remembered she had said he was an old vampire, though she had never told me he was *that* old. I remembered something about his liking the sea, which was a detail I probably would have forgotten if not for the investigation into De Laurentis.

He must have *called* her. It wasn't something all sires could do as strongly, but an ancient would have a lot of command over his fledglings. It must have been a year ago, which was when she had changed and dropped everything. This was the only thing that made any sense, except it didn't make any sense at all!

I wanted to talk to a vampire about it, but it was still light out. They were all asleep. The bastards.

I considered calling Moore but decided to wait on that, too. That was purely social idiocy, really. No, instead, I decided to finish cleaning my apartment.

When I was putting books back on my bookshelf, something fell out of my copy of *Great Expectations* and clinked against the tile floor. I frowned and bent down, picking it up. Once I saw what it was, I dropped it again.

It was a cameo. One of those pendants with the profile of a woman's head in white. I knew what they were called now.

"Damn it!" I shouted at no one in particular, and then said it a few more times until the words stopped making sense, and I sunk into myself.

Well, at least now I knew who ransacked my place. I guess I kind of knew that before, though.

☾O☽

I called Moore down at the station, but she wasn't available. I didn't feel comfortable talking to anyone else, so I left a message to have her call me back.

After that, I'm not too proud to admit I spent the rest of the day wallowing. Some of it was spent trying to think on my cases and take notes, but I had trouble focusing. That might have had something to do with the fact that I was still hung-over, but it was also just because I was overwhelmed and couldn't escape it. I had to take a little time to regroup and get my sorry self back together.

Once it was dark, I made an odd choice, and I went to the office. Madison looked surprised when I walked in.

"Is Sadie expecting you?" she asked, blonde brows drawing down.

"No." I sat down on the couch.

She looked around. I didn't know what she was looking for. Maybe she thought there was a hidden camera somewhere and this was a prank of some kind. I slouched in my seat and watched her. Madison St John wasn't the kind of girl who hid her feelings very well, so her confusion and suspicion were very obvious.

I was still looking at her when she turned back to me. "Why are you here, then?"

"I've been asking myself that same question since I pulled into the parking lot." I shrugged. "I didn't want to be alone?"

"So, you came in here?" She still didn't look like she believed me and, really, could I blame her? Until tonight, I had made it pretty clear I needed to be dragged through the front door by a team of oxen, and even then, I'd make them work for it. Now, I sat here of my own free will looking for company.

I sighed. "I didn't really have anywhere else to go." I had hoped it wouldn't come out nearly as pitiful as it did, but I don't think a phrase like that has any hope at all of not sounding absolutely pathetic.

Madison appeared to hear it the way I hoped it didn't sound and looked guilty. Why did she look guilty, I had to wonder? It wasn't her fault. "I don't imagine it will be very interesting here," she said after a moment. "I have to pay the business's bills. Our landlord insists we pay our rent this month."

She made me smile more often than I let her know. She was kind of infectiously happy, which was probably why I tried to avoid her. "I won't be in the way."

Her eyes darted around again, looking for the hidden camera I guessed, but when she didn't find anything, she looked at me. Now I wondered if she was trying to guess if I had lost my mind. I was wondering that, too. If she found an answer, I hoped she'd tell me.

My phone rang. It was Myles calling for a status update. I gave her the shallowest summary I could because I wasn't ready to tell her just how deep it had all gone.

When I hung up, the door opened, and Stanton walked in. She lost a step when she saw me, almost falling on her face. "What are you doing here?"

"You know, for a place of business, you guys are not at all welcoming," I muttered, second-guessing being here, and yet, even as I did, I couldn't make myself get off my ass and walk out the door. Didn't I have murderers to catch? But no, I sat here feeling awkward instead.

"She didn't want to be alone," Madison supplied. "I think she likes us more than she admits." Her lips curved up at the corner.

"I never said *that*." I had an image to try to uphold, but after this, I knew the thought was a stupid one. I think my image was already done for.

Stanton chuckled and nodded, and for some reason decided to sit down beside me. The mirth wasn't in her eyes anymore. "Are you having trouble with the turn in the case?"

I looked between her and Madison, and I might have wondered how much Madison knew, but she probably knew all. I didn't imagine there was anything the one knew that the other didn't. They were like freaking conjoined twins sometimes. "I guess you could say that," I confessed.

Her expression was very serious. "You have hardly

talked to me much in the months you've been working here, or with us I should say, but I've figured out a thing or two. I know you're religious. I'm not, so it feels weird to say this, but have tried praying on it?"

That surprised me, and I knew it showed. I didn't know how to reply to that, and I wondered how she had come to it so quickly when I hadn't thought of it. That was shameful of me, I realized. "I..." I stopped, finding myself at a loss for words.

The phone on Madison's desk rang. Both mine and Stanton's heads snapped toward it, the sound shattering the moment of silence. The wolf looked apologetic as she answered it, but then frowned with pronounced irritation.

"May I ask your name, sir?" Pause. "I'm sorry, but I don't give out information like that to people who don't give me their names and their reasons for calling." Another pause as she listened, and her eyes turned to me. I knew instantly it was another call trying to get information about me.

I jumped to my feet and tore the phone out of her hand. "Who the hell is this?"

"I'm just looking for some information." It was a man's voice. He sounded rather frightened. There was something familiar about him, but there was too little said, and I was too angry to figure it out.

"Why are you trying to get information about me?"

"This is...Dakota?"

"Yes, damn it, and I want some answers!" I was all but screaming into the receiver. I was tired of this shit. "Tell me who you are!"

The line clicked and went dead. I squeezed my eyes shut and handed the phone back to Madison.

"I have to go." I turned and fled.

CHAPTER FIFTEEN

I took her advice, and I went to church.

I sat in the empty sanctuary of Adelheid Episcopal, and I meditated on the chancel area, realizing in the chaos of my life recently, I had stopped remembering the little things that had kept me sane before. It's funny how that works, isn't it? You forget the things you need the most just when you need them most.

Bowing my head, I folded my hands and closed my eyes. I whispered my prayers.

"*Vater Unser im Himmel, Geheiligt werde Dein Name, Dein Reich komme. Dein Wille geschehe, Wie im Himmel, so auf Erden. Unser tägliches Brot gib uns heute, Und vergib uns unsere Schuld, Wie auch wir vergeben unseren Schuldigern. Und führe uns nicht in Versuchung, Sondern erlöse uns von dem Bösen. Denn Dein ist das Reich und die Kraft und die Herrlichkeit, in Ewigkeit. Amen.*"

When I was done, I opened my eyes and looked up again. "God grant me strength. God grant me wisdom. God grant me endurance." I asked for the same three things I had asked for since I was a teenager. I wasn't sure if He was listening anymore, because my life seemed to have turned into a huge joke at my expense, but I had to hope.

I had to have faith and not forget again.

My phone rang on my way out. I hurried outside so I wouldn't get yelled at for talking on the cell in the church.

"Dakota," I said, stopping on the sidewalk.

"It's Samantha Moore. I got a message that you called me, so I was returning it, although we'd been getting ready to call you anyway."

"Really?" The plural in that was what made it bad news. "What's going on?"

"Lucy Fitzwilliam is missing and probably dead, but we don't have a body." It wasn't good news. It sucked to be right sometimes. "Her place looks like McNamara's did. There is evidence of a fight and blood all over, but the body was taken before we arrived. We have another journal with the same writing."

I scrubbed my hand through my hair. "Do we know anything else?"

"There was a security camera in the ATM across the street that captured images of Stone and Rau walking in. They must have left through the back, because we don't have anything of that." She sounded reluctant to tell me. I guess I couldn't blame her. I didn't seem to have any blame to put around on anyone but me, and *them*.

I didn't reply right away. What could I say? It had been good of her to tell me, but I knew they didn't need me on this. It was a cop matter, and less and less of it was in my hands, it seemed.

A thought came to me rather suddenly. "What's the name of the night guard at the ME's office? The one who was on duty when the body went missing."

There was a delay before the reply. "Nina Parker, but we saw her being hypnotized on the tape, and we didn't find anything about her that connects her to anyone."

"I got a funny feeling. Can we meet at her place? Do you have an address?"

"I probably shouldn't give you that information." She sighed and gave it to me anyways. "We will meet you there.

Be careful, and don't do anything foolish."

"I promise."

☾◯☽

Parker lived in a first story apartment in a building on the south end of town. I parked on the street in front and sat in the car for a while, looking at the window I believed would be her place. There was a light on, so I assumed she was home, but I didn't hear any sounds of a fight, and there were no bodies making shadows in front of the window. So, I kept waiting a while longer, watching.

My patience, such as it was, paid off when I saw Carrie walking up to the door.

I got out of my car and took to the sky, silently flying and descending behind her as she rang the buzzer. It was polite as any guest might be, but I knew what she was there for. I didn't understand what was behind it, but the pattern was clear.

"Hello, Carrie," my human mouth said as I shifted behind her.

She flinched and turned to face me. I caught a glimpse of a tattoo on her neck, but I couldn't focus on it. "You know I can't let you take me in without a fight, don't you?"

I wished she would. "It would be easier for you if you did. I don't want to do this. I don't like having to do this."

"But I've left you no choice." She smiled resignedly.

Nothing else had to be said. Her fist flew at my face. I managed to avoid some of it, but a vampire's glancing blow still snapped my head to the side. She got behind me and wrapped one hand around my throat, whispering, "I should have known that you would find me. You were always too damn good."

Reaching over my shoulder, I grabbed her head in both my hands and threw her over my shoulder. She hit the door and slid to the concrete. "You put up a good chase, love." The word slipped out and tasted bitter.

"I knew they'd send you after me." She winced as she straightened onto her hands and knees but did not stand. Instead, she threw herself at my legs. I jumped in time to miss the hit, but she was already on me when my feet touched down again. "You're better than this. You're holding back." Her knee jammed between my shoulder blades as she drove me to the ground.

I knew she was right. It was one thing to chase after her without ever seeing her face, but another to have to hit her.

Cursing, I shifted into a snake and slithered out of her grasp. I didn't want to do this, but she was right. She had left me no choice. Coming to my knees in human form, I spun and kicked her in the shin. She shrieked and went down. I lunged for her and got her. Her hand clawed at my side, and I didn't realize right away that she tore a chunk out of my hip, and there was more to the wound than I immediately knew.

Hauling back, I slammed my fist into her jaw with all my strength. It flattened her. Cracked the bone. She wasn't quite conscious or unconscious, but she was immobile.

"Why did you do this?" I demanded as I pulled enchanted handcuffs from my pocket. It stung as it touched my skin, my silver allergy no less than any other supernatural being's, but not enough to burn. I snapped them on her wrists as she groaned thickly.

Right then, the cops showed up. Moore rushed up to us with Marlowe and Johnston close behind. I let them take her.

"May I present Carolyn Stone," I said with no small amount of sarcasm.

"Thank you," Johnston said with a crooked smile as Marlowe led a swaying Stone to the car. Only her state would let a human like Marlowe control her, but before she recovered entirely, she'd be in the car and then in the station's cell. The silver in those cuffs would weaken her, but speaking of being weakened... "Dakota, are you okay?" He sniffed the air.

I opened my mouth to say yes but looked down and saw a considerable gush of blood flowing freely down my thigh. There was a burning and tingling at the edges of my senses that told me she'd had silver on her. How the hell did she do that? Silver-tipped claws or some bullshit? How did I miss that?

"It seems I'm a little injured." My voice sounded distant to my ears.

"Shit, Dakota, we should get you to the hospital."

I shook my head stubbornly. "I just need to get home. I'll heal soon enough with some rest." I hated hospitals. I'd been injured worse than this and healed myself.

Moore put her hand on my arm. "Don't be an idiot."

"I'll be fine." I laughed weakly. "I just need to go home."

Her eyes were such perfect indicators of what she was feeling when she wasn't being The Cop. She didn't like the idea, but she didn't think she could make me do anything, and she was right. I'd bet even weak with blood loss, I was still stronger than her. "Well, you're sure as hell not driving yourself home." She reached into my jeans pocket for my keys.

I couldn't help but laugh, though it was more like a snort. "And you didn't even buy me dinner first." I said it quietly enough that only she heard me, and her deeply tan skin darkened a little in the cheeks, but she didn't reply, just turned and hauled me by the arm to my car.

The other cops were taking care of everything. Moore took me home.

☾○☽

By the time we reached my apartment, I felt feverish. My chest was a little tight from the effect of the silver, but it wasn't bad enough to convince me to go to the hospital. I didn't even want Moore's help getting into my place, but she didn't give me a choice. She helped me in, through the still-broken door lock, and onto my bed. (My couch still didn't have cushions.)

She pulled a little knife from her pocket and cut the side of my shirt, carefully peeling away blood-soaked cloth. The silver slowed my healing. The bitch had silver, my God, how fucked up was that? I was barely aware of what Moore was doing. My brain was just in such a fog, and everything hurt. Vaguely, I knew she was cleaning the wound, but there wouldn't be much to do other than press something to stop the bleeding and wait for my healing to do the rest.

Once she was done cleaning, I knew that the wound was very slowly beginning to knit itself back together.

"Thank you," I murmured. I couldn't make myself look at her, feeling the way I was, so I stared at my ceiling.

God grant me endurance...

"Do you need anything?" she asked.

I shook my head. "You don't have to stay. I'll be okay." I didn't want her to stay and see me like this. I didn't want her to go.

"Like hell." She didn't hesitate. "Johnston and Marlowe will have things locked down at the station. Someone needs to make sure you don't keel over."

I would have laughed, but I couldn't find it in me. I would have cried, but I didn't have that in me, either. We were silent for a while, instead. Words slid in and out of my brain. I became less and less conscious of what I was saying. I knew what I was saying, and yet I was only barely aware of it. It was one of those strange states of being that is very hard to describe.

"Do you know how long I've been alone?" I closed my eyes to try to keep the world from spinning.

"No." Her hand slid around mine and held me here.

"My sister left me in eighteen-eighty-three. I didn't know she was…as she was…till the nineties, but I hadn't seen her since eighteen-eighty-three." I didn't mention the other. That had been long before. My brain still held that back. I don't know why. "I've been alone since then."

She squeezed my hand. "What about Carrie?"

I laughed weakly. "She made me happy, for a while. I don't know if I ever really let her in, or if I wasn't alone. Can you stop being alone when you're only with a person for a year? I spent two hundred with my sister before she left me."

"It's a long time."

Cold swept over me, and I shivered. She let go of my hand, and I was sad for the loss, but she only moved to pull a blanket over me and sat on the bed next to me. I leaned my head against her leg and sighed.

"Tell me about your family," I whispered.

"What's to tell?" She asked the question, but I could hear the warmth. "Boston Irish, my parents are Catholic, and my whole family is crazy. There are six of us kids."

"There were six of us." I didn't know if she heard me. She didn't press if she did, but she rested her hand on my shoulder.

"I'm the first one to show any paranormal ability, so you can imagine how that freaked out my rather traditional family. My liking to date women didn't help any, but they love me, and they've found a way to make peace with both parts. They don't like it, but sometimes I think by now it's just because I'm less likely to give them grandchildren. Still, it's not like my brothers and sisters aren't doing a good enough job of that."

"You're not just Irish," I said.

Moore laughed softly. "You're right. My grandmother on my father's side was Japanese."

That explained a lot about her exotic good looks. It was an interesting mix. Even with my eyes closed, even though the haze, I could vividly see her face.

"Do you love them?"

"Of course I do," she replied. "They drive me crazy, but I love them a lot."

"That's good… A family should love each other…"

I was drifting off. I fought it.

"Go to sleep, Dakota," she whispered. "I promise I'm not going anywhere."

"Don't promise that." Sleep was claiming me. "Everyone leaves."

❨O❩

The year is 1628.

It has only been three months since it happened, but Erik and I have been doing our best to survive and make sure our little sister survives, too. We went back to the village, pretended to be other things, but they are dead. Our family is dead, and we are alone.

Guilt has been eating away at me since that day. I sit on a log with Erik while Hannah sleeps. We are in human form, which we don't spend much time in these days.

"Erik," I whisper. I can't meet his eyes. "I have something I need to tell you."

"What is it, Anneliese?" He is all concern as he takes my hand. We are all that we have left, after all.

Tears are thick in my throat. "It's my fault." I finally meet his eyes. He doesn't understand, at first, but then it becomes clear.

"How is it your fault?"

No longer stuck in my throat, the torrent of emotion is freely flooding my cheeks and so hard that it is spattering on my knees. "I was running in the forest, like a wolf, like..."

"Like Mama and Papa told us not to!"

"I know!" I cry. "I couldn't help myself. The animal was too loud, and I had to run. I needed to get out and get air, but I saw some men in the woods, and I panicked. I tripped, and I lost my form. I became human, just for an instant, but maybe they saw me. Just a day or so later, they came for us!" I cover my face with my hands and try not to wail miserably, because I don't want to wake Hannah up.

"Anneliese," he breathes, "how could you? Our parents are dead! Lukas and Hilde and Dagmar are dead! They killed them because they thought we were witches, which was why you were told not to shape change!"

"I know." I beg him to stop. I have already said all of this to myself. "What do you want from me? I can't take it back! I can't change the past, no matter how much I might want to!"

He gets to his feet. "I have to... I have to get some space." He walks away.

"Erik!" I hiss, trying to get his attention and make him come back. "Erik!" I see him shift into a bear, taking after Mama, and lope deeper into the woods.

We don't see him again.

Chapter Sixteen

My head was clearer when I woke up, and my side was again whole. The tiny bit of silver in my system had worked itself out, and I felt like I might just live after all. That was, if I survived the embarrassment.

Somewhere during the course of my time asleep, Moore had also drifted off. She was still sitting up, leaning back against my headboard while I lay next to her with my head still against her leg. Oh, good God. Had I made a complete fool out of myself? I pushed through hazy recollection and decided that maybe I avoided being a total idiot, but I still felt pretty embarrassed.

I slipped off the bed as carefully as I could, and she didn't wake up. I grabbed clothing off the floor that I had worn sometime in the last few days. Getting stuff out of the dresser or closet would be too noisy, so I just changed into whatever smelled okay. I wanted to let Moore sleep and give myself time to recover my emotional equilibrium.

Plus, I was starving. Healing and working out the silver had put a hell of a strain on my system. As great as it was, it needed food and sleep to power itself. I got the latter, thanks to Moore, but now I needed to take care of the former.

Fortunately for me, I lived above a restaurant, and the smell of Chinese food lured me outside. Hunger fogged my brain the way my injury had before, and it kept me from thinking about all the things I didn't want to think about, like Carrie and my sister and whoever was stalking me. That last one ended up being particularly inconvenient to forget.

I was coming back upstairs with enough food to feed me, Moore, and a small Midwestern town when I realized I wasn't alone in my little corner of the night. I mean, I knew Moore was upstairs, and there were people in the restaurant, as well as the occasional car passing by, but this was particular. It was the hairs on the neck feeling.

"Don't be afraid, please," the voice said from the shadows.

"Really? This seems like a moment to be afraid." Of course, I didn't feel afraid. I felt pretty pissed. I also felt silly confronting a shadowy stalker with food in my arms, but there it was. "Who the hell are you?" I recognized the voice from the phone, and I hoped for a better reply than the last time.

I could make out the shape of a man, but he knew what he was doing. I couldn't see anything of his face. "I'm sorry that it has been like this." He did sound sorry. Something tugged at the back of my mind, something...familiar, but I couldn't pin it down. "I didn't want to upset you. I just had to find you."

I wasn't feeling any better, but I had a strong feeling he wasn't planning on hurting me. If he wanted to attack, he would have done it already. "You're sounding like a celebrity stalker, but I know I'm not that famous. Why won't you tell me who you are?" The fact that he wasn't attacking me made me less keen to attack him. Or maybe I was just still tired.

"I just want to help."

"Help?" Now that was an unexpected word. "You could help me a whole hell of a lot by telling me who you are!"

"I..." He stopped.

Upstairs, the door opened, and Moore came out. "Dakota?"

The man bolted. I couldn't tell where he went. He

seemed to slip in between the shadows.

"Dakota?" Moore asked again, starting down the steps. Apparently, she hadn't noticed him, and I wondered if I had hallucinated the whole thing.

"Yeah," I said, going up the stairs. "I, um, got food." It was amazing how I managed to hop from pissed-off adult to awkward teenager in the space of six feet.

"Good idea." She stepped back and let me walk in, shutting the door behind us. "How are you feeling?"

I smiled, setting the food down on the table. "I'm better, thank you. I'm all healed up." I rubbed the back of my neck. "Look, I got really weird when I was hurt. I'm sorry if that was strange for you. I'm not very good at apologizing, I don't do it very often, but I feel like I should at this point."

Smiling, she seemed really at ease. She didn't seem bothered at all, and that bothered *me* on some level. I didn't know how to handle that. "It's all right, Dakota, really. I don't—"

I interrupted her. "Anneliese," I said, surprising myself. "My name is Anneliese. It was the name I was born with. I don't know why, but I'd like to hear you say it. I haven't heard anyone say my name in more than a hundred years." I smiled weakly. You'd think that after being alive all this time, I'd be better at things like this.

"Anneliese," she said gently, resting her hand on my arm. "You were pretty badly hurt, and you got hit with silver. It's all right that you got a little crazy, and it wasn't like you got that bad in the first place. You talked. You let the walls down a little, and that was okay. You asked something about me, and that was okay, too. You kind of became a little more human, and while I know you're not, I mean it in a good way."

I laughed sheepishly, having to look away. "How old are you?"

"Thirty-four..."

"I'm older than you by more than three hundred and fifty years," I said, "so how is it that I feel like a teenager here?"

She smiled, sat down, and started sorting out food. "We all get that way sometimes. Sit your ass down and eat."

☾○☽

We ate a meal together and talked like normal people once I got over myself. I started finding it hard to believe I'd pulled the shit on her I had, because she was a really good person and had an amazing way of disarming me. She also made me not think about the bad stuff without having to feel bad to do it. I told her about the guy outside, and she was suitably worried but agreed with my estimation.

I knew we'd have to get back to work, and soon, but it was nice while it lasted.

Work decided when we started up again by the ringing of my phone. "I'm seriously considering shooting this thing," I muttered as I answered it.

"It's Johnston," came the voice from the other end, "and shit is weird down here. We have been questioning Carrie since she recovered, and she's been totally stonewalling us. Now, she says that she will talk, but only to you. She's willing to confess, if it can be you."

"What?" I wasn't sure I'd heard him right.

"I know, but she wants you, and she has signed a waiver that confessing to you will be the same as confessing to the police, but that's what she wants, and we want her to fess up, so please get down here as soon as you can." He paused. "And if Moore is still there with you, tell her to come, too. If Carrie says anything about Rau, she'll want to know." He hung up.

I didn't want to talk to Carrie. I was done with Carrie. I'd done what I was supposed to do, what I was paid to do, and now I was done. But leave it to Carrie…

Turning to Moore, I relayed the conversation to her. She was surprised, too, but we got moving. After cleaning up, we headed right out. We took my car since hers wasn't there, and we didn't say much during the drive. I was too busy trying to figure out what Carrie was doing and why she was demanding to talk to me.

When we arrived, Johnston came out to greet us. He didn't have anything new for me as we walked to the interrogation room. Stanton was in the observation room, and I wondered why she was there. Apparently, the question was on my face. It was a good thing I didn't have any poker games to play.

"I thought maybe you could use a friend after this," she answered the question I didn't ask and smiled.

"Oh," I said. My brain wanted to cave in, so I moved right on. "Can I go in and get this over with?"

Johnston nodded and opened the door for me.

Carrie sat there, looking remarkably placid. Her face had healed, and they'd apparently given her a washcloth because the blood was gone, too. Her hands were folded in front of her, held in place by cuffs chained to the table. She looked up when I walked in and smiled, the faint points of her teeth flashing. "I wasn't sure you'd come."

"You didn't leave me much choice." I yanked the chair out and sat down. "So, I'm here. Talk." I was determined to not give in to whatever this was.

She shook her head and laughed quietly. "You always were a hardass. Well, fine." She looked down at her hands. "I'm sure you've figured it out by now, but my sire called me to him over a year ago. He is an ancient. I couldn't refuse his call or what he told me to do."

"Who is your sire?"

"De Laurentis."

I nodded. I'd already known that, but I had to get her to say it. "What else did you want to tell me?"

Carrie didn't reply right away. She sat, perfectly still, like the dead. It forced me to look over her hair, which I always thought was pretty, and to mourn the way things had gone.

"I killed them all. We fought, and I killed them." That was direct. "I'll give the detectives the details."

I knew she had done it. I had been after her myself, but hearing her say the words still made someplace deep inside hurt with a sharp pain. "Why did you do it, Carrie?" My voice was barely above a whisper, but I knew she'd hear me.

She inhaled slowly. "I can't tell you that. I can tell you everything you'll need to know to prove I'm telling the truth, but I can't tell you why."

"Why not?" Motive wasn't necessary for a guilty verdict, but it sure helped. It would help *me*.

"My sire is powerful," the words escaped on her breath. "I can't tell you without risking going crazy, and I can't bear the idea of that, for any amount of time. He has commanded me, and I must obey." She looked up and met my eyes, and I knew she wasn't lying.

That was damn frustrating, but I knew it wouldn't do any good to push. "Did you know she was my sister?" I had to ask.

She smiled apologetically. "Yes, almost immediately. As soon as I saw her abilities, I knew, even though you never told me much about your past." She paused. "Not that you two are anything alike. That woman is cold in a way I've never known, and that's saying something. I was sired by a bastard."

"His command doesn't keep you from calling him names?" I couldn't keep from smirking.

"No, amazingly, it doesn't," she agreed with a faint hint of humor in her eyes. "He's too arrogant to think that anyone would do that, so he doesn't even try." Leaning back, she shook her hair over her shoulder. "I'm sorry, Dakota. I really am. I never would have chosen things to turn out this way, but I didn't have a choice any more than you did. But I still love you. And I hope the best for you. It's over now."

There was resignation in her face that I had never seen in her before, a sorrowful wisdom that made everything hurt. I couldn't even ask. "Carrie, I..."

She held up a hand. "Don't say anything. We're done here. I've said what I wanted to say, and now you can send in the detectives for me to write my statement. Thank you for coming to talk to me."

"Right." I got to my feet and started to walk out.

Her voice reached out and grabbed me before I made my escape. "They've named me Brynhild." She sighed. "I know what's coming."

I turned to ask, but she wasn't looking at me, so I kept walking. I went into the observation area and found them all there. I knew they'd been watching and I felt exposed, not unexpectedly. Johnston didn't bother waiting for me to say anything, and I didn't bother trying to say anything. He walked into the interrogation room.

"Are you okay?" Stanton asked. Moore lingered in the corner, but she watched me closely. They both did, and I wanted to tell them both to knock it the hell off, but I couldn't find it in me to do so.

"Yeah, I'm all right," I said. I did find it in me to do something slightly unusual when I said, "Thanks. I'm going to head out. I'm done here."

If I thought I was going to get away that easily, I was sadly mistaken. My phone rang. It was Myles.

"I just wanted to call and say good work on Stone," she said. "Thank you for closing the case. I got word from the cops just a few minutes ago."

"Of course. It's my job, after all." I hoped she wasn't going to bring up why this had been a little more than my job. Before I could dash off the call, I remembered a small detail I'd heard about Rikki Myles once, about her support group. "Can I come see you?" I couldn't believe I hadn't thought of it before.

"Sure." She sounded surprised. "I'm in the office for a little while, but then I have a meeting."

"Good."

☾O☽

It didn't take me long to get there, and she met me in the front office, which was empty for the moment.

"You look awful." This was the first thing she said.

I laughed. "Thanks, I got in a scuffle with Stone and got injured, but I'm healed up now and just need some more rest and whatnot, but in time. I wanted to talk to you about your support group and a rumor I heard once."

That stopped her in place. "That was unexpected. What rumor?"

"That you all... Well, how to put this...something about Amazon warriors?" I hadn't put any stock in it before, but after the Thorson boys and everything else, I had to give it a shot.

"Before I acknowledge or dispute anything, I need more than that." She smiled.

I racked my brain. "That you all are reincarnated Amazonian warriors, like Hippolyte and her girdle?" I did know *some* of my mythos.

Myles stared at me for a while. I wondered what she was thinking. If I was wrong, then she probably thought I had gone entirely around the bend. If I was right, well, I might need to think the same thing about her, but then again, I was kind of hoping. If she was indeed that crazy, it would be a crazy that could help me. At that moment, I could use all the help I could get, so I hoped for crazy.

"Drive with me to my meeting," she finally said.

I followed her out of the building and into her car. Neither of us said anything until she was on the road.

"Yes, you heard correctly. No, we are not in need of psychiatric care." She glanced sidelong at me and smiled slightly before turning back to the road. "It happened to all of us after we fought cancer and won. Each of us had a mastectomy. Surviving made us feel like warriors, and the loss of the breast was compared to Amazonian warrior women. We don't believe we are literal reincarnates, but that the spirit of it is in us. It helped us survive."

That was a more sane and long-winded speech than I had expected. "That's pretty heavy." I knew I sounded like an idiot, but there it was. "What do you do with it now?"

She shrugged. "We're a support group, a community, a family. We help each other and we try to use our group to help people. We try to do good works."

"Anything else?" I asked, feeling genuinely curious.

"We aren't fighting any wars, but we do work out and keep in good shape. We also study military tactics that are close to what we feel are our roots. Amazon women chopped off one breast to better fire their bows. We do archery. We train in ancient weaponry and strategy and stuff like that."

"Does it have any real-life applications?"

She chuckled, turning into the parking lot of the community center. "We do some live-action roleplay to amuse ourselves, but we just do it, and if the skills are ever needed, they'll be there. Otherwise, it just helps keep us strong as a group. It's a bonding thing."

I tried to imagine it: having a family like that, which

wasn't your real family. "It sounds nice," I said thoughtfully.

Myles smiled. "It is. Why don't you come in and meet folk?"

At first, I was going to say no, but then I remembered that she'd driven, and I would have to walk home if I didn't. So, I followed her and sat in a room amidst a lot of stories. Some people talked about the past, what they had been through, and some people talked about the present and the future.

It was an enlightening experience, and the way they talked made it pretty obvious how strong the bond between them was. I was envious. I didn't know how much time passed, because I wasn't watching my watch. I was just listening.

And then I was listening to my phone ring. I slipped out of the room, ready to throw the thing into the nearest wall, but I answered it anyway.

"Bad news," Moore said.

"I don't want to know."

"Somebody broke Carrie Stone out of jail."

CHAPTER SEVENTEEN

"*What the fuck happened?*"

Having a vested interest in the case, Myles had been kind enough to drive me back to my car so I could drive tensely back to the damn police station, storm in, and start shouting at people.

The detectives were standing in a triangle of crossed arms and angry faces. Stanton was back again, I imagine either because she was stalking her boyfriend or because of the PR angle, and she didn't look any happier. She just wasn't one of the points of the triangle.

"We don't know." Johnston was growling. It brought to mind his tiger half. "She was here, and then she wasn't. She became a damned ghost for all we know. We have security all over this building. We *are* security! Yet, she's gone."

I saw Stanton reach out and slip her hand inconspicuously into his, and he growled again, forcing himself to sit down.

"I've been hunting this woman for days, and it nearly killed me. Once I brought her in here, you were supposed to keep a grip on her!" I was thirty seconds away from either waving my arms in the air like a lunatic or turning into some kind of wild creature and tearing out the nearest throat. This was ridiculous.

"We know." Marlowe was far more deadpan, but displeasure was clear in her face, too.

I reined in my more beastly instincts and folded my

arms over my chest to keep my hands away from someone's throat. Just thirty minutes ago, I'd been sitting in a room that lifted me up, and now I was here. "So, what are you doing to find her? I've done my job. It's your damn turn to catch her sorry ass."

No one looked very sympathetic. "We're doing what we do." Marlowe frowned at me.

"We'll catch her, again," Johnston said.

Stanton watched from her seat on the edge of someone's desk. Her dark eyes looked thoughtful. "The quicker the better, obviously," she offered, but her tone was quiet. Her tone sat in the background as much as she did. "We know De Laurentis used his abilities on one guard already. We're interviewing everyone between the front desk and the cell, right?"

"Yeah," Marlowe replied. "There aren't many, and I already talked to them, but if they were put under some kind of power, then an interview isn't going to do it. Point of fact, I don't think we'll be able to tell without something more concrete, like a video. The tech guys are working with the security system to see where things went awry."

"I don't suppose we have any idea *when* she went missing?" I asked.

"Moore went in there about twenty minutes ago and found her missing. It was some time before that," Johnston was the one to answer this one.

The phone on his desk rang. He answered it but just listened. And if I had thought that his face was dark before, it got darker pretty quick. He dropped the receiver back on the cradle and sighed. "We know where Carolyn Stone is."

I felt something go cold inside. "Where?"

Did I really want to know?

☾O☽

She was still outside De Laurentis's house in Infinity Park when we got there.

The path here had started as a call to 911 to report a fire. The fire, it turned out, was feeding on the bushes in front of the house. At the center of the fire was Carrie's body, just far enough in to not be burnt before they came to put it out. After they had, they called the cops. The uniform recognized Carrie's face and called us. Now, here we were.

I looked at her with great pain, lying there with her hands spread to either side, face up to the sky and stake in her heart. She lay on top of the bushes, and the stake was so long that it pinned her to the ground. Even for a vampire, there was no coming back from this. It was all over.

They let me under the crime scene tape, and I wanted to go touch her, just to prove to myself that it was true, but I knew I shouldn't. I kept myself back, wrapping my arms around my body as if warding off a chill, even though the air was warm and the heat haze from the fire still lingered. The acrid smell of smoke on the air just made it all hurt worse.

"It had to be De Laurentis and Hannah," I said quietly.

"One or both," Stanton agreed. She stood beside me. I am not sure why she had come, but I didn't mind her presence. Maybe she was there in case the press showed up. She shivered. "I know *he* was here at least."

I looked at her. "How do you know?"

Returning my glance, she replied, "I can feel it. An ancient can't keep from leaving some traces of themselves behind, and other vampires can feel it. It's one of the reasons ancients have so much power and control in our society." She smiled darkly. "Because they have great power and control. No vampire could meet an ancient and not know it, not feel it, and be controlled by it to some degree."

"It would be worse if it was one's sire, right?"

She nodded. "Quite a bit." She brushed long strands of dark hair out of her face as she stared at the house. "His energy is all over the place, and if he lived here, it would be, but this is fresh. It was left very recently."

Now, I frowned. "You can tell that?" I knew I didn't know everything when it came to vampires, but I had never even heard of this.

"Yeah, I can. All vampires can, but many aren't very good at it. The strength of the ability varies, but you can get better with time and effort. My own sire was very good at reading the traces left by other vamps and..." Her voice caught, and I knew this was a sensitive subject for her. "She taught me."

I guess you learn something new every day, and it kept me from thinking about Carrie's body lying there. For a minute, at least.

"When will they move her?" I asked after there was a long pause between us. Some moments, I couldn't bear to look, and at other moments, I couldn't bear to look away. The religious imagery was not lost on me, and I had to wonder if that was my sister's doing.

"Soon." Stanton's voice was gentle. "They have to make sure they didn't miss anything. They need to record the body *in situ.*"

I smiled mirthlessly. "You sound like you're dating a cop or something."

She laughed softly. "You pick up a few things here and there. It comes in handy."

There didn't seem to be any disagreeing with that, having just found it useful myself, so I didn't say anything else for a time. Stanton stayed with me. The investigators all did their investigating, but I felt like a solid point in the middle of a storm. Everything was going on around me while I stood still.

"I don't understand." I sighed. "Why break her out of

prison just to kill her? She couldn't tell us about his reason, and he'd know that. So, why go through the trouble?"

"Maybe they were punishing her in some way. Because she got caught?"

It was as good a theory as any.

One of the uniforms came up with a plastic bag. "This was found on her body," she said, "and Detective Johnston said to show it to you, Ms. Dakota, in case you knew what it meant."

Frowning, I took the bag. Inside was a ragged piece of paper with the word 'Repent' scrawled on it. I recognized the handwriting. It should have hit me harder, but I was too dead now to notice.

"It means what we already know," I said flatly, handing the bag back to her. "It means Hannah is involved, and she hates her sister. Johnston will understand."

The uniformed officer frowned but didn't want to ask, so she nodded and walked away.

Repent. Was it my fault Carrie was dead? I sighed deep in my soul and remembered something she said as I was leaving the interrogation room.

I turned to Stanton. "Can I leave? I mean, you don't need me for anything."

Stanton eyed me for a moment, like she wanted to ask more but didn't and shook her head. "You're free to go. We'll call you if anything turns up." A pause. "You gonna be okay?"

"Yeah, I'll be fine." I forced a weak smile and turned, walking away.

Moore caught up to me before I even got in my car. I looked at her. "Don't you have, you know, work to do here?"

She shrugged. "They're afraid you're going to do something stupid and asked me to babysit you."

"Oh, please." I snorted and got into my car. Maybe a

week or two ago, I would have gunned it before she could get in. Now, I didn't. She got in, and I drove back to my place.

"I'd say one of these times you're going to have to buy me dinner, but then again, you already have," she said as we got out of the car.

I looked at her over the roof with a frown. How could she be cracking jokes at a time like this, when I was like this? Or even, dare I say it, flirting? But when I met her eyes, I understood why and how. I'm not sure I appreciated it or not, but I didn't *not* appreciate it. I didn't reply, and we walked into my apartment.

Letting her settle as she wanted, I sat at the table and got out my phone. My computer was gone, after all. I got on the internet since I still had my router.

"What are you looking up?" She sat beside me and peered at my phone.

"Carrie said something when I was leaving tonight. She said they named her Brynhild, and she knew where it was going to end, or something like that." I typed in Brynhild and read what came up. My frown deepened with every moment.

"What's it say?"

"Brynhild was a Valkyrie who was sent to Earth to decide a battle. She knew who Odin, king of the Norse gods, wanted her to pick to win, but she chose the other. Odin punished her by sending her to live as a mortal woman, where she slept in a castle in the mountains, surrounded by..." My words stumbled for a moment. "Surrounded by a ring of fire until a man would come and rescue her and marry her. And there's more about the lover being tricked and marriages and murder and, well, sounds like an old tale."

Moore leaned back in her seat. "So, are you thinking that Carrie was left in a ring of fire as punishment for choosing the wrong one?"

I dropped my phone onto the table and folded my hands

in front of my mouth. "It sounds like a possibility." My voice wouldn't rise above a whisper. It was me. The note, that one word, had said as much. It had to be me. She must have done something, and this was their message.

My throat tightened, and I got up to get a glass of water.

This had all seemed like such bullshit, but whatever I thought of it, it was all pretty damn real to them. I thought of the Thorsons. My thoughts skipped around for a while as I drank the water until I thought of the journals that had been found.

I got my files and pulled out the copies. "I wonder if the Thorsons could tell me what these say."

"I guess there's one way to find out."

☾O☽

It was Matthew Thorson who answered the door this time. Now, I noticed the way every other house was surrounded by green while this house was surrounded by dead plants like it was winter.

"We haven't done anything!" This was the first thing he said and in total exasperation. "We can't find him, okay?"

"Good, don't even try." I walked past him, and Moore followed. He sighed and shut the door. I handed him the papers. "Do you know what these say?"

Frowning, he took the papers and shuffled through them. "Some of it," he replied without much delay. "The handwriting isn't very legible, so some of it will take a while to be sure, but I could tell you a little." He looked at us. "Where did you find these?"

I exchanged a look with Moore. "In the homes of people that have been killed. They were journals."

He looked markedly green around the gills and sat

down. "Murdered people?" He inhaled slowly. "Did Njord do this?"

"Not directly, but sort of." I didn't know how much I should tell him. "I think it was Skadi who had the bigger hand in it, and one they'd named Brynhild."

"Brynhild," he repeated. "The Valkyrie?"

I nodded.

Thorson sighed and shook his head. "That certainly doesn't bode well for her."

"No, it didn't."

After a moment, the meaning of my words dawned on him, and he took on that green shade again. Swallowing his stomach down so loudly I could hear it, he looked at the pages. "I don't know how much I can tell you from these. They are like, well, like journals. They are just thoughts being jotted down. I see notes about times and training schedules, things like tactics and weapons." He paused and straightened, reminding me of a meerkat I saw on the Discovery Channel once. "Vanaheim."

"Didn't you say that was where Njord had set up his new shop?" I asked, remembering the names. I couldn't spell them very well, but they were memorable.

He nodded. "We haven't been able to find it, even though we've been trying. There are clues to its location in these, though." Thorson flipped from page to page and back again eagerly. "It's the east side of town. They talk about a graveyard that's right beside Vanaheim, one of the original graveyards from the city's founding."

Now I perked up. "That could only be Adelheid Memorial. The east half of the city has the most forest, and it's certainly the oldest corner. It has the only original cemetery. There's a house there, a huge house."

Up until this point, Moore had been lingering watchfully in the background. "Don't go there, Mr. Thorson." Her voice held an unmistakable note of warning but not threat. Threats were usually my job. "De Laurentis and Rau have already been a party to several deaths. You don't need to find yours there."

Thorson shook his head quickly. "Oh, I have no intention of going anywhere near the place." He hesitated. "But, if you could, we need Mjolnir back."

She arched a brow and looked at me. I gave her a 'I'll explain later' wave. "We can't make any promises," she said, "but we will at least see them all to justice."

He looked like he wanted to argue, or maybe just to beg, but he didn't. He handed the papers back to me, looking utterly defeated. I didn't know what to tell him.

Moore seemed to know better than I did. "Thank you." She smiled at him, and it appeared to make him feel a little better. "Is there anything else you know that might help us in apprehending him?"

"No." He didn't hesitate. "It's been over a year since the split in the group. He could have done any number of things by now. The Valkyries are probably very different than how they were when they were with us. We don't know what Mjolnir does but keep Asgard living. I don't know how many more followers he might have. Only about twenty-five went with him."

"There are that many Norse gods?" I interjected.

He shook his head. "We don't all believe we're gods. Some just feel the call of the people and follow the gods, so we are all part of the same community." He sighed. "I can at least say that he didn't get many of the other gods to go with him."

I was probably going to hate myself for asking, because it felt silly to have the words come out of my mouth, but I asked, "What other gods did go?"

"Thankfully, not Aesir."

Our blank looks were question enough.

He sighed. "You never studied any mythology?" He went on before we could answer. "The Norse gods were either aligned with the Aesir or the Vanir. The Aesir were warriors, and the Vanir were of wisdom and fertility. Funny that the Aesir now want peace, and the Vanir are warmongering." He shook his head. "Njord was a Vanir god. When he split, he took Freyr with him. He was most important of the Vanir here with us, and Freyr is the son of Njord. Not biologically now, but metaphysically. Watch for him, and be grateful his sister has not yet been reborn. There aren't really any others worth mentioning, though."

I was back to being sure this guy was crazy, but on the other hand, I was a four-hundred-year-old woman who could take the shape of any person or animal I wanted. I guessed I only had so much room to talk. He could be right.

"I hope you caught all that," I said to Moore, and then started to leave. I heard her thank Thorson again before following me out.

Once outside, I was talking again. "We need intel. Despite what anyone might think, I'm not stupid enough to go charging into any and every situation imaginable without a plan. I don't know what to think about everything he just said, but I know that it's a group of people that could be any size, being led by two incredibly powerful beings in my sister and an ancient. We need to know more about what's going on in there right now before anyone considers going in."

We got into my car. Moore listened patiently until I shut up. "I agree, but what do you suggest? I doubt we can place a phone call."

I knew what I had in mind, but I didn't like it. It seemed… really wrong, but it was the only idea I had. I just had to hope that the police would agree to it.

Chapter Eighteen

Sarah Beaumont looked distinctly uncomfortable as we walked into the morgue.

Carrie laid on the stainless-steel table. The ME hadn't even had time to start the Y incision when the police had called him and told him to hold off. Johnston had been open to my idea once I had explained it.

"Are you sure this is okay?" Beaumont asked, looking at every instrument like it was going to bite her. "I'm not used to working in a place like this."

"Would you be more comfortable in a graveyard?" I sounded dubious and I knew it, but it seemed damned strange. And I liked thinking about that oddity more than about Carrie lying naked on that table, waiting to be cut open and prodded from the inside out.

She turned to me. "Actually, I would. That's where I usually work. It's familiar." She didn't sound upset by my asking, or embarrassed. It was just fact. "But I can work here, too. It's just really strange."

Beaumont was the animator for the Stanton Agency, which meant she made zombies for a living, but not the kind in the movies that chase people down and eat their brains. She had complete control over them, at least enough to keep them from running off or attacking anyone, but the raising never lasted long. Only a necromancer could do more than that and, thankfully, those were rare. Animators are more common, but Beaumont was prodigious. She was the only seventh-generation animator I had ever met. Quite frankly, I was surprised the line hadn't bred into necromancy by now.

She walked up to Carrie and looked her over. "At least she's not rotting," she commented. "I've raised some that were little more than bits, just enough bits to talk. It's unpleasant."

I winced to hear her talk about Carrie like that, but she didn't notice. Moore was there, being The Detective, but briefly touched my arm.

"Let's get this done." Beaumont inhaled deeply, closing her eyes for a moment. I supposed she was meditating, finding her center or something like that. When she opened her eyes, she looked at us. "I've only done a few vampire raisings. I'm not sure why, but they don't last as long, even for me, so work fast."

I nodded.

In the best example of her abilities, she performed no ritual. She didn't even touch the body, although she held her hand just over Carrie's forehead. I felt a tingling run up my arms and down my spine, and I knew her power was at work. I was surprised she didn't glow. And when I heard Moore's shivering inhale beside me, I knew she felt it, too.

After a few moments, Beaumont moved her hand, and Carrie sat upright. It was a freakish thing to see her like that. The stake had been pulled out, but the hole remained. Even I felt a little ill when I saw it.

She turned her head toward me. The motion was slow and laborious, but she smiled, and I thought I saw something even in those glassy eyes.

"Siegfried," she whispered. "I knew you'd come for me."

The reminder of the Brynhild story wasn't one I needed, especially to put me into it. I had been avoiding that. Briefly, I closed my eyes. "Carrie," I said. I tried to make my voice louder, but it was difficult. "If I'm right, now that you're dead, the command your sire gave no longer has any power of you, right?"

Her smile deepened, even if her gaze seemed to go straight through me. "I knew you'd figure it out. What do you need to know?"

"Why did you do it?"

"Skadi decided that no woman may become a Valkyrie without being worthy and without being powerful. To prove herself worthy, she had to fight me. No human could win, but if she did well enough, she was kept. If she was kept, she was turned."

Moore stepped up beside me. "So, you're saying that all the Valkyries are vampires?"

Carrie's head pivoted toward Moore. "Yes. Roughly a dozen. They are trained in ancient weaponry before we even fight to prove worthiness, and then there is more training after. They are warriors. What's more is that Freyr is a witch. I don't quite understand his power, but he has made it so that they do not sleep in the day, as long as they avoid the sun."

"Twelve fucking vampires who can fight with weapons almost no one these days knows," I said slowly. "And we lose the advantage of a daylight attack? Fuck me."

A wicked glint flickered through Carrie's eyes, I swear it did. It creeped me out.

I grimaced and tried to distract myself. "What's the tattoo?" I had seen it on McNamara and on Fitzwilliam and now on Carrie.

"Magically infused to not heal over. It's *ansuz*, the ancient Norse rune for the All-Father. Odin. He who commanded the Valkyries. It's put upon all the Chosen Ones, the ones who will be tried, the ones that wish to become Valkyries. Those who pass the test keep the mark."

I shivered and sighed.

"How many followers does De Laurentis...does Njord have now?" Moore seemed to sense my difficulty and stepped in. I was grateful for that.

"Besides himself and Skadi, Freyr is with them. Three lesser gods. Thirty human followers, but some are just children. However, he has found Fenrir and Jormungand."

"Oh, my God!" I exploded. "What the hell is with this shit?! I need a damn score card to keep track of it." I spun around and took a few steps away. I couldn't take it anymore. It was all too ridiculous! Yet, here I was.

"I know it's hard for you, Dakota." Carrie was still talking behind me, and to me, but I couldn't turn around. I couldn't bear to look at her like that anymore, or at least I needed a freaking break. "Believe what you will, but these are dangers you'll face. You need to know. Fenrir is a great wolf, more than a wolf. He is not a shifter but is big and mean. Jormungand is a great serpent. He is not so big as he was, cannot encircle the world, but you'll never have seen anything like him. These are beasts he has in Vanaheim."

"When did my life become this?" I asked no one in particular, too quiet for anyone to hear.

"She doesn't have much longer." Beaumont was still there. I'd almost forgotten.

I swallowed it all down. "Do you know what Mjolnir does? Can he use it?"

There was a quiet rasping sound, which I realized was Carrie laughing. "It infuriates them both beyond reason. All it's done so far is given us great flowers, but they cannot make it do anything more than be a hammer. I think they have considered doing home repairs with it. It is a big weapon, dangerous on its own if you have the strength to wield it, but no power they can access. It is Thor's, and only he may bear it."

"Thor," I snorted. "What about the layout of the place?" I had to think tactically. It helped.

"It's all darkness, for the Valkyries. There is a giant hall when you first enter, so great that it is practically a house itself. There are corridors with rooms, which are where the followers stay. Then another room and another great hall. Njord likes the great hall, but everyone else moves around. There is no second story and no basement, and no electricity. It's all torches and candles and fireplaces. There is, strangely, only one door in."

"Sounds delightful," I muttered. I knew we didn't have much more time, but it was hard to think. She had told me some very disturbing things that were going to affect our plans, but all I could think about was that hole in her chest.

Finally, I forced myself to turn around. I wanted to cry and felt like I might come close, but it still held off. "Thank you, Carrie," I said miserably. "You've been a lot of help."

The light faded from her eyes. "Good luck." Then, just like that, she unceremoniously fell back against the metal bed, and we were left with a strange silence around us.

In the quiet, I offered a silent prayer for her soul.

☾ ◯ ☽

We commandeered an interrogation room.

It was Johnston, Marlowe, Moore, and I. Moore and I had told them what Carrie had said, and we all looked... concerned.

"Twelve vampires with swords?" Johnston asked. "We don't have the manpower or the power to take that on."

I could almost see wheels churning in his amber eyes. He was trying to figure out how to make this work. Only a shifter or another vampire was powerful enough to go hand-to-hand with a vampire, and there weren't twelve of them on the payroll. Even silver bullets wouldn't do it. And we couldn't just go in during the day when they were in the vampire coma.

"Plus, De Laurentis and my sister," I pointed out, "and apparently a sorcerer with some power, a couple scary animals, and thirty humans."

"Humans will respond to guns, at least," Marlowe pointed out, "but we'll be screwed when it comes to the rest."

I sighed, staring at my hands. "I can take Hannah, and I think I can take De Laurentis if I can get him alone. And she didn't say the animals were bulletproof." I tapped my fingers against the tabletop. My mind ran like it was lit on fire, searching for every angle. I didn't like what I had to do, but I liked having to work. "She said De Laurentis likes to be in the great hall, perhaps I can get there and find him on his own."

Moore tapped my calf with her toe. I looked at her. "You can't know that," she said. "What if you find both him and your sister? You'll be overwhelmed."

I appreciated her concern. "If they are, I can try to get a shot off. A silver bullet should at least slow Hannah down and let me handle De Laurentis. Silver is just as hard on us. You saw what a trace of it did to me."

She still didn't look like she liked it but didn't say anything.

"What about the vampires, though?" Johnston asked.

"I have an idea for that, but I don't think you're going to like it." I smiled humorlessly.

"Hopefully, it's not as creepy as your last idea." Moore leaned back in her seat and put her hands behind her head, sighing forcefully.

I shook my head. I didn't know if it would work, if they would agree, or if the cops would allow it, but it was the best I had. "The woman who hired me to catch Carrie runs Myles Bails-Bonds. She's part of a unique group of women who believe they are...imbued, for lack of a better word, with the spirits of Amazon warriors. I know it sounds crazy, but it makes sense when you listen to them. They don't think they're gods, but they are obviously all special. Even the humans have a powerful quality to them that normal humans don't. I've met them. And they train in ancient weaponry. They know tactics and have armor for it. There's at least a dozen of them."

"I don't know if Captain Roy or the court would like the idea of civilians fighting our battles for us," Johnston pointed out, but he wasn't saying no.

"The best I have is that Myles is licensed in the bail business. She's a bounty hunter, with the preternatural license that allows for certain special circumstances, so if we said these women were working for her…"

He caught on fast. "They'd be hunters, too, of a sort, with the special privileges that come with the job." Inhaling deeply, he shook his head slowly. "It'll be sketchy, but we could make a case for it under the circumstances. I think this is the definition of extenuating."

Marlowe also shook her head. "This sounds like deputizing a posse in the old west."

"Ain't far from it," I said, "but I don't know that we have a choice. We have a thousand-year-old vampire and a strong shifter on a power trip with a growing cult following and a dozen vampires at their disposal, and I do mean disposal. We know where they are now, and we need to act. Lives are certainly at stake."

"No one is disputing that, Dakota." Johnston's voice was soothing as he held up his hands. "I'll talk to Captain Roy. You talk to your friend and see if we can get her on board. If she'll agree, and I can get the captain around to it, then we'll make preparations and go round us up some bad guys." He even managed to smile.

Chapter Nineteen

"**I** can't believe you got them to agree to this." Myles stood with her arms folded over her chest, shaking her head.

Things were unfolding with blinding rapidity. Johnston had made his case with Roy, and I had made mine with Myles. Admittedly, my job had probably been easier than his. Now, we were all in the basement of Myles's house. This was an odd place to begin a police operation, but that's where the Amazons' gear was.

The cops and I were outfitted as much as we were going to be, namely with our training and special abilities and guns. Everyone but Johnston had Kevlar, though I didn't think we'd need it. All of us were equipped with silver bullets. We discussed last-minute strategy while the Amazons got into some wicked-looking archaic armor. I couldn't help but wonder, in between the moments of discussion, where the hell they got it.

"The Amazons look like they know what they'll be doing," Johnston, who was the point man on our little expedition, began. "When we find the Valkyries, we set them loose. Marlowe will be in charge of the uniformed officers we'll have with us who will be arresting the human followers. Now, you all remember every word I'm saying because I'm going to shift before we go in there, and tiger mouths are not known for their grasp on the English language. I'll be looking for the animals and at least keep them busy while you two—" He looked at Moore and I. "—go on ahead to the great hall and find De Laurentis and Rau. Arrest them if you can, but do whatever it takes to bring them down. We can't fuck this up."

That was an understatement, I thought, but I didn't say it.

Looking to my left, I watched one woman strapping a breast plate into place. It gleamed dully in the light of the basement.

From somewhere in the middle of the group, someone started singing. It was odd, at first, but bizarrely compelling. More so as the others joined in, still putting on their armor and acting like this was an everyday occurrence.

The tune kind of lilted along in a language I didn't recognize, but I could feel it. Like it was when Beaumont raised Carrie, there was a strange sensation along my skin, but this wasn't like anything I had ever felt before. One of those moments that found its way inside you, located your soul and squeezed, yanking it upward until you felt like it was going to pull you right off your feet.

When they stopped, I felt like I'd been dropped on a floor of ice. The detectives, even Marlowe, had a similar look, but Myles just smiled and hefted her shield. "We're ready."

Everybody piled into a few vans for the short field trip across town where we parked down the street from the Vanaheim house, which had been under surveillance since we learned the address. (That was Moore's doing.) By all accounts, no one had left, and we had to assume everyone was home.

We snuck up to the house like a police procedural movie. The only difference was a pause outside the van for Johnston to strip naked and shift into a huge-ass tiger. I had yet to see that in a movie, though these days, it wouldn't be long.

Every window was boarded up, and there was only the one door, so that's the way we had to go in if we wanted to keep the element-of-surprise as long as possible.

What we met once through the door was darkness and silence. The cops got out their flashlights, but torches on the walls crackled to life as we slowly walked down a long corridor. I went first with the detectives, the Amazons in the middle, and the cops to the back.

I had my gun out, held like the cops. It was an unusual feeling for me, but it had a range that even I couldn't attain with my shifts.

As we stalked forward, I realized I was anxious. It wasn't a feeling I'd had a lot in my life in the past few years, until recently, and I didn't like it. It was too close to helpless. It was too close to out of control, or at least it stripped away the illusion that I had any control in the first place. It tightened my chest, made my heart hammer, and my body break out in a slow, cold sweat.

No, I didn't like it at all.

We left the passageway and found the giant hall Carrie had told us about. Giant did not even begin to cover it. It was massive. I couldn't see the ceiling properly in the torchlight, and there were tall stone columns. It was like we had left New England entirely and fallen into some castle that could not possibly exist in the United States. The country was too young for places that looked like this, but here we were.

From the far end, a rhythmic metallic banging began. I didn't know what it was, but Myles shared a strange smile with the other Amazons.

"This one is us," she said.

The women all slipped between the detectives and me, fanning out in a long line. I could smell the vampires coming toward us, the lingering odor of the grave drifting toward me, and now I could see dark shadows emerging from the black. It was some of them, though not all, that were making that noise. They were banging on shields.

Vampires spread out to match, woman for woman, the Amazons. It was surreal. I saw Myles smiling, and she shouted something across the hall in an archaic language even I didn't recognize. One of the vampires laughed and replied in the same or a similar language, and I still had no idea what they were saying, but it was obvious. Two armies of old shouting friendly insults at each other, before they tried to kill one another.

I'd never forget this moment. It was too strange.

Myles laughed like the vampire had before, and then they all leaped at one another. It was a blur of motion and a crash of metal. It was more deafening than any cinematic portrayal had ever managed. I watched as an unfamiliar vampire collided with Myles's shield and was rolled off it, driven to the ground, but on her feet again before the Amazon could drive her point home. Everywhere else in the hall was blurs of silver and bronze. A spectacular flashing of skill and speed and stubbornness.

It mesmerized me, and I would have stayed and watched forever if someone hadn't nudged me. I didn't even know who, but we kept moving. The Amazons well and truly kept the Valkyries busy while we slipped past them and crossed the length of the giant hall. The sounds of ancient shouts and clanging metal followed us as we emerged into the next set of corridors, lined with doors that started to open.

"Humans," I announced with a quick sniff of the air.

Marlowe gestured for the uniformed officers to begin rounding them up. They emerged from their rooms into waiting sets of handcuffs. I knew that would be the only easy part of the evening.

Meanwhile, Moore, the tiger, and I kept on.

God grant me strength. God grant me wisdom. God grant me endurance.

I waited any minute for something to jump out at us.

Tapestries hung on the walls, and I waited for something to come out from behind one of them, but nothing did. There were only sounds behind us, and nothing to either side. There was nothing ahead until we reached the end of the hall and found a door.

"What the hell is that smell?" I couldn't miss it as we drew near, but I had no idea what it was. It wasn't like anything I had smelled before.

"Let's go find out," Moore said as she moved forward to open the door.

She didn't get very far. What I had been expecting finally happened, and I was so overwhelmed by the smell, and apparently so was Johnston, that we didn't hear the man coming. Or maybe it was done by sorcery, because I somehow just knew that, when the lanky redhead came out from behind the tapestry, we were looking at Freyr.

Moore was the closest. He dropped a shoulder and knocked her to the ground, but she had a heel in his kneecap before he could jump on her. We started to move, to help, but she wasn't having it.

"Go!" she shouted. "I got this!"

He crawled toward her, but she lunged forward, cracking his head to one side with her elbow and kneeling on his chest with her gun in his face. Whatever psychic abilities he had did not compare with some good old-fashioned ass-kicking.

I went for the door, and Johnston and I went through.

On the other side was, without a doubt, the biggest fucking snake I had ever seen in my life and the bastard dog I'd chased down several days ago. Apparently, he'd been broken out of jail too, because there he was. There *they* were. They were both somehow chained to the wall, but with leads long enough to reach us. We barely dodged out of the way in time.

Johnston ended up on Fenrir's side, and I got the snake.

In all of my life, I'd never fought a snake before. I had escaped *as* a snake, but I had never fought against one. I had no instinct for this, so I retreated to what was familiar, which was my cougar form. The gun really didn't seem like it was going to do me any good, and I knew a human form wouldn't help, so mountain lion it was.

The snake, Jormungand, was on top of me before I realized it. I scrambled out with the benefit that it had no arms or hands, but my claws scrabbled at the stone floor and getting away was a narrow thing. I whirled around and leaped onto it, grabbing it with my claws on either side, trying to dig in, trying to bite, but the scales were like metal, and I couldn't get through.

It writhed and slung its body from side to side. Without any purchase, it flung me off, and I hit the wall. It hurt like hell and made stars fly around my head. Dimly, as I briefly lay dazed, I was aware of the sound of a cat and a dog fighting on the other side of the room. I saw Johnston hunkering down before launching forward, swatting Fenrir's head with a massive paw, and then leaping four feet into the air and landing on the wolf, jaws diving for the jugular as the wolf spat and snapped.

The stars faded, and I was aware of Jormungand coming for me but was slow getting back on my feet. I realized maybe I shouldn't have worried about De Laurentis and Hannah because the fucking snake might just do me in.

Glass and wood shattered above my head and sprayed the shards all over me. Both the snake and I looked up and saw what I couldn't believe: a giant bear had broken through the boarded-up window and landed on top of the snake. Apparently, the bear's teeth were better than mine because the snake hissed as its flesh was torn. The bear mauled the thing while it fought, trying to coil around its new enemy. The bear...

The bear... Mama...

Erik!

I was floored, but I didn't have time to be. Erik—because I could smell it was him—tore one final bloody chunk loose, and Jormungand flopped to its death. There was only one look shared before he lunged to help Johnston's stalemate against Fenrir, but I knew what it meant: keep moving.

Im namen des Vaters...

CHAPTER TWENTY

I burst through the door into the final great hall, like in some video game where you reach the final level.

What I saw brought me up short.

De Laurentis sat in what could only be called a throne, with one arm dangling over the side while his legs hung over the other, like some power-drunk prince. I suppose that's what he was, too. Or, should I say, what he *had been*.

His head was hanging back and half-gone, caved in by some massive force. Long hair hung down, clinging to bits of what remained of his skull and clotted with dried blood.

I didn't know what to do. I didn't know what was going on.

Hannah walked out from behind the throne. She had a massive hammer in one hand and blood spattered from hand to neck. "He was a pompous creature." She laughed so easily, like it was the funniest thing in the world as she trailed her fingers over his hair. "I knew this wasn't going to last, but he thought it would be fun. I suppose he was right."

She looked exactly like she had when we were children, with a heart-shaped face, pale skin, and long blonde hair in a single braid hanging over her shoulder. Only the clothes were different, and I knew she had taken on this appearance for a reason. She had to have known I was coming, and this would be it.

One of us was going to die today. I honestly didn't know

who it would be.

I had shifted into a human form without even realizing it and taken on the appearance I had worn as a young woman, before our world had ended.

"Why, Hannah?" I asked her the question I had never had the chance to. The one that had burned in my mind for more than twenty years. "Why did you do it?"

She could have toyed with me and made me spell it out, but she didn't. She knew exactly what I meant. "Why not?" Casually, she swung the hammer over her shoulder and gestured grandly with her other hand. "For centuries, the humans have had all the power. We lived cowered in fear that they might learn what we are. But do you know why they killed us? They feared us because we are the powerful ones. I got tired of hiding and running and crawling on the ground just to survive, so I could bow and scrape before an *inferior* race. I refused to do it anymore." She licked flecks of blood off her lips and spat. "Giovanni, as he was called then, was powerful. He was eight hundred years old, and he felt like I did. The Thorsons and their silly little group just offered gullible minds to use as we wished. We used our power to do what we wanted and to take it out on those who would persecute us. How can you blame me? You watched our parents chained and carted off, so you saw what humans are like very early."

"It was the fault of a few, not the entire race," I said, but my voice and my argument sounded weak. "It didn't give you the right."

She eyed me. "You're such a disappointment, big sister. You could have been so much more. You could have been powerful. You could have been *great*. You and I together could have become a force that none could reckon with." She spat again. "Instead, you chose to wallow for decades and lower yourself to them. What, to punish yourself?" Hannah tilted her chin up, looking down at me. "I know you think it was your fault. I heard you talking to Erik that night, even if you thought I was asleep."

That hammer might as well have been thrust into my stomach. I might have asked if that's why she did it, but she stayed with me for two hundred years more. The two could not be connected.

"I will give you...absolution before you die, big sister." The smile on her face made every cell in my body go cold. "It wasn't you."

"What do you mean?"

Hannah laughed again. "Oh, you were always so dense. What a martyr you are! I think you liked blaming yourself, because it made it easier than blaming that which you had no control over. I think you *liked* scrambling for survival, so you could *repent*. But guess what, Anneliese, it's all been for nothing. It wasn't you that gave us away. It was me. I told them our parents were witches."

There are no words to describe what I felt in that moment.

"Why?" The same question kept coming up.

"I was mad at them." She shrugged and crossed in front of the throne, leaning back against the blood-free arm rest. "I didn't know they'd take *all* of us."

I laughed because it couldn't be true. This couldn't be true! I pressed the heel of my hand against my forehead. "Not only did you let me spend those two centuries thinking it was my fault, but you turned over our entire family to be slaughtered and burned because you were mad at our parents?" I repeated it out loud to see if it could possibly make more sense, but no, no, I couldn't believe it. "*Hexe!* Were you always soulless?"

She shrugged. "The argument has been made that we're all soulless, so maybe I am."

"No." I shook my head. My blood boiled. I wasn't anxious

anymore. "No, I am *not* soulless. I might not *like* people, but I still follow the teachings of our youth. I still remember what our parents taught us, and *I* still have the soul God gave me. I don't know what happened to *you*."

"Maybe you should ask God when you see him," she mocked, "which should be very soon. Or maybe the Devil. Go to Hell, Anneliese."

"You first, little sister."

We leaped into the air at the same time, taking to wings to the tune of the hammer falling from her no-longer-hands. No matter what else, we were not entirely dissimilar. Two hawks vying in the wind, we grappled claw-to-claw with one another and shrieked. Our avian screams echoed the torrents of our brains as we spun, wings flapping haphazardly as we crashed to the ground.

Neither one of us would want to give an advantage to the other by shifting first, but birds could do nothing on the ground.

She broke and shifted into a wolf. It had been the form we'd worn the longest at one time in our lives. Hannah tried to grab my feathered body in her teeth, but I was too fast, the bird no longer there when her jaws closed. Instead, I was again the mountain lion. I shrieked and jumped forward, knocking her off her feet as I got to mine.

We paced. We stalked. We moved in a slow circle, eyeing each other and waiting for the moment. The moment when the other would jump. The moment when we had an opening. We growled, long and low. The sounds had changed, but the words were the same.

This time, I broke first and leaped at her. I knocked her off her feet, and we tumbled side over side in a tangle of fur and claws. She snapped at my neck. I lunged for her jugular. Neither of us got any more than glancing bites.

Then she did something I didn't expect. She shifted to

human.

"Anneliese," she said piteously. And even as my brain screamed that it was a trap, I couldn't move. I had my baby sister pinned down, and my human side reasserted itself, pushing the beast out of the way. But then she smiled and surged forward, knocking me on my ass. Getting her hands around my throat, she squeezed with her great preternatural strength.

I coughed and choked. I had stumbled but refused to give up. I wasn't going to die today, and I got my hands on hers and pulled. We were evenly matched, and the muscles of my arms trembled to pull her hands away. I didn't have the focus to shift. I could only pull as she struggled against me. My brain was light on air now, and it made it harder.

"Why won't you just die?!" she screamed. Her hands were still close enough around my neck to try to bang my head into the stone, but I would not let her. The world swam at the edges, but just as I readied myself for one last exertion, I watched a great stone hammer swing from seemingly nowhere and catch her in the side of the head. She flew off me and skidded several feet away, dead in an instant.

I gasped and dragged air into my lungs, looking wildly to see Moore standing there with Mjolnir in her hands. She looked at Hannah for a long moment and, confident she wasn't getting up again, moved to me. I stared at her, and then I stared at my sister.

It was over. It was...over.

Moore knelt beside me, wrapping one arm around my shoulders, pulling me to her because apparently, she saw what was coming before I did. I pressed my face to her shoulder.

And I cried.

CHAPTER TWENTY-ONE

It had been just over three days, and everyone had given me a lot of space. Everyone except Erik.

No, he's Edward now.

I laid back on my new couch and Wagner's *O Fortuna* blasted in my apartment as loud as I could get away with without my landlord shouting at me over the phone, or in person when I didn't answer her calls.

For these past three days, I had spent a lot of time thinking and trying to keep it from descending into wallowing, though it did anyways. On the upside, the Amazons had been victorious. Despite the odds, none of them had died, although a few were still in the hospital. Two of the vampires had died, but the rest had been arrested. It had turned out better than I could have hoped for. Johnston had been beaten up, but his shifter healing had taken care of that in a couple days. Thank God, or Sadie might have killed me.

Vanaheim had been cleaned out by the time my brother and I limped into the night with Moore alongside us.

I had spent the next day switching between hugging my brother and yelling at him for stalking me and, as I learned then, for hiring that P.I. to trail me. He had said he didn't know how I'd react and had been afraid I wouldn't forgive him for abandoning us, for spending decades angry, and then the rest of the time afraid before he came to find me. I supposed I could understand, but I was still pissed off about the tactics. Kind of. Mostly I was really just happy to have him back and happier that he was going to move to Adelheid to be near the only family he had left.

It was enough to make me forgive him. Mostly.

Now Edward was kneeling on the floor next to me on the couch. I hadn't been able to get rid of him, after all, but it wasn't like I'd really tried.

"How are you feeling?" he asked.

"I think I might be okay, in a few more days," I replied, turning my head toward him. "I still don't believe any of it, you know? I chased her for twenty years, but until we were standing there, it always felt so abstract. Like I could distance myself from it. Now, she's dead. Now, I know what she did to our family. I don't know how to feel about that."

Resting an elbow against the cushion, he put his chin on his hand. "Give it more time, Anneliese. After all, it hasn't been that long. Even twenty years isn't that long, for us."

I laughed quietly but without much mirth. "I guess you're right, though some things I don't know if you can ever come to terms with."

There wasn't much to say to that, so he didn't try, but after a moment, he went on to something else. "You have a visitor. Detective Moore is on our doorstep, and she says you're not getting rid of her this time."

"You left her standing outside the door?" I sat up. "Jesus, apparently the bad manners are hereditary." I smacked him against the side of the head as I pulled myself up and went to her.

I hadn't exactly been avoiding Moore, but I hadn't wanted to see much of anyone. I had a lot going on, and everyone seemed to understand that.

"Hi," I said with a half-smile. "I'm sorry my brother is a jackass."

"It's all right." Her smile was a whole one. "I bet it's nice to have a brother to say that about."

I laughed. I wasn't used to being this jovial for this long. I hoped it didn't last, because I couldn't handle it. "It is. It really is. Do you want to take a walk?"

She nodded, and I stepped out to meet her. I left Erik to do whatever he wanted. I could have said the walk was to keep him from eavesdropping, but with people like us, he could just shift into a pretty little butterfly and float along behind us. I'd never suspect.

"Thanks for everything, Moore," I said after we'd walked for a while, meandering down the sidewalk.

"Moore?" She laughed. "I think you should probably call me Sam after all of this." She nudged me with her shoulder. "I'm heading back to Hartford tonight. It's not a long drive, but I've been staying with Detective Marlowe, believe it or not, and I think I've just about worn out my welcome."

The capital was only about an hour away, but it still seemed like a really long distance after having her practically at my heels for a few days. "Will we see each other again?" I asked.

Sam glanced sidelong at me. "I hardly think you're going to get rid of me so easily."

☾○☽

A couple of days later, I learned that Mjolnir had been returned to its rightful owners after being released from evidence. I drove by the Thorson place, but no one answered the door when I knocked. There was, however, a note tucked into the windowpane. I almost missed it, but it had my name on it. I opened it curiously. It simply read: *Thank you.*

I smiled a little and couldn't help but notice the place was in bloom far beyond what could have been expected, especially considering what it had looked like before.

It made me wonder.

☾O☽

This time when I went into the office, Madison didn't look around for any hidden cameras. She smiled.

"How're you doing?" she asked. I had been asked that question more in the past seven days than the past seven years, I thought, but somehow, I didn't mind. I'd mind again soon, I was sure, if it kept up. But for now, I was content. Well, maybe not content, but I was okay.

"Hanging in there. Is Stanton in?"

Madison bounced to her feet and peeked her head into Stanton's office. Then she came back and nodded at me. "Go on in."

I stepped through the door and shut it behind me. Stanton tilted her head curiously. "This must be some kind of record for the number of times you've come willingly into the office in so short a time."

"I could leave." I dropped into a chair.

"At least you haven't lost your sparkling personality." She smiled, though. "I'm glad you came by. I was going to call you." She opened a drawer and pulled out a box, handing it across the desk to me. "Vance wanted me to give this to you. Said I was more likely to see you first. I told him he hadn't been listening to me when I bitched about how little we saw you in the office."

Giving her a dry look, I took the box and opened it. Inside was my mother's knife. I kind of just puddled up inside. "Thank you," I said softly. I seemed to be getting better at that. I stared a moment longer before closing the box and setting it on my lap.

Stanton gave me the moment I needed before she went on. "So, what can I do for you, Dakota? What brought you in?"

I inhaled deeply, recovering myself and unable to

believe I was about to ask this, but here it was. "I think you need to teach me how to be…more of a team player."

She didn't reply right away. "Is this some kind of a joke?"

Snorting, I rolled my eyes. "Make this easier on me, would you? I guess I got a lesson in humility the past two weeks. I can't do it all alone, and you all are good people. Most of the time. I knew it when I first met you, Stanton. It's why I helped you. It's why I agreed to this. I…" This was painful, and getting the knife back drove the point home, so to speak. "I know I haven't been the best person to be around, but I want to at least try to work with you guys better, and I think I'll need your help to do that."

"I feel a little like a nature expert, trying not to startle the wildlife," she commented, sitting up straighter in her seat. "I would like that. And I would be glad to help. Though, by its nature, your profession tends to be one that has you working alone a lot, but I imagine we can do better at integrating you anyway."

"That would be good." I nodded, and then forced another moment of gratitude. "Thank you."

I knew this feeling of love for mankind wouldn't last, but maybe I could make things a little better before it faded. It was quiet now, but it wouldn't always be. The beast would always be in there, but maybe now I had the upper hand.

Maybe.

Author's Note

Dakota… Dear, dear Dakota… She has been one of my favorites since the very first word I wrote about her. According to my mother, Dakota is who I would be if I "said everything that came" into my head. She's probably right. Less trauma, thankfully, but no less snark.

This book is pretty much the same as it was when I first released it eight years ago, which is a nice thing because it means I got it mostly right. And who doesn't like being mostly right, yeah? Her story has always been one of my favorites, as she is, so you'll see a lot more of her in the rest of the series. There is no getting away from her!

Outside of Adelheid circa a few years ago, I sit at my computer and write this note for the re-release while we are still on mostly-lockdown thanks to Covid-19. It's a weird world we live in now, and that's quite a thing for the author of the world of Adelheid to say, isn't it?

As I write these words, I hope that everyone who reads this book—now and in the future—can find an escape from their own lives for a little while by living in the heads of the characters in these stories. They may have their own struggles, as we all do, but they always overcome and grow, as I hope we all can.

If you want to know more about the town of Adelheid, the people who live in it, and the lore I chose to use when writing these preternatural species, you can check out my series wiki at wiki.authorkbthorne.com.

Sincerely,

K. B. Thorne, August 2020

About the Author

Born a Connecticut Yankee in nobody's court, K. B. Thorne grew up to brave snow and talk fast.

She started reading when she was three and never looked back, soon frequently falling asleep with a book under her cheek. At eleven, she discovered *Night Mare* by Piers Anthony and entered the world of grown-up fantasy fiction. As you can guess, it was all over from there. She started writing at fourteen, then met vampires as a teenager and the concept for what would become Adelheid (now the Blood Rights Series) was soon born. Mia Darien followed a few years later, and the books were released.

However, K. B. is also a third-generation Trekkie. Somewhere in a vault at Paramount is a very angry letter written by her grandmother when *Star Trek: The Original Series* was cancelled, so sci-fi is in the blood too. Alongside a love of love and an adoration for her first love of epic fantasy.

K. B. Thorne is the evolution of Mia Darien after years of learning and living. She has taken both of those things to become a smarter, better writer with a fresh new face and take on the literary world. Thorne writes the urban fantasy, fantasy and sci-fi, while Sadie Johnston writes the romance.

These days, when she's not desperately trying to find time to write, she works as a freelance editor/cover artist/formatter and happily lives her unconventional life alongside her very own Named Man of the North and their mini-tank. (Who is, you know, their son.)

You can find K. B. at authorkbthorne.com!

OTHER BOOKS BY K. B. THORNE

Writing as K. B. Thorne
Blood Rights Series

Bad Blood
Blood and Thunder
Blood Moon
Written in Blood
Bloodshot
First Blood
Out for Blood
New Blood
Flesh and Blood

Out for Blood Series
Bones & Blood

Bellator (Anthology)
Good Things (Anthology)
Ashes to Sunrise (Anthology)
The Shape of Tomorrow (Anthology)
Born of Defiance (Anthology)

Writing as Sadie Johnston (Romance)
Beauty
Help Wanted (with Viola Dawn)
Threnody (with Alastair Malone)
Here, Kitty Kitty (Anthology)
Amor Vincit Omnia (Anthology)
Second Chances (Anthology)